Acclaim for *The Lives of Rocks*

"Quietly powerful." — *New York Times Book Review*

"Mr. Bass's writing is smooth and direct, without false start or stumble . . . He's a true master of the short story." — *Dallas Morning News*

"*The Lives of Rocks* digs deeply into the geology of the human condition. [These are] highly polished gems to be turned over in the mind, again and again." — *Seattle Times*

"Rick Bass's strong, moving, and impulsive stories make an important world that is all his own. Physically specific, emotionally universal, *The Lives of Rocks* raises the level again on Bass's already urgent and valuable work." — Thomas McGuane, author of *Gallatin Canyon*

"Few writers evoke nature as well as Bass . . . the depictions he offers are resplendent." — *Boston Globe*

"Bass is at his best like this: graphic, unrestrained, thrilled at a beauty even chaos can't diminish. His best is rarely out of sight in the collection." — *Washington Post Book World*

"Rick Bass is one of a dwindling handful of American fiction writers still celebrating the importance of place, the natural world, and the struggle of a few brave souls to live and work respectfully in what's left of our western wilderness. . . . *The Lives of Rocks* is his most lyrical and powerful book to date . . . a masterwork."
— Howard Frank Mosher, author of *On Kingdom Mountain*

"Bass is a master of this form and it is a delight to have these stories from the borderland." — Doug Peacock, author of *Walking It Off*

"A sterling collection of ten graceful stories connected through Bass's invocation of elemental forces, but at the same time each is deliciously distinct." — *Publishers Weekly*, starred review

"Compassionate and hard-hitting, knowledgeable and transcendent, Bass is essential." — *Booklist*, starred review

The Lives of Rocks

STORIES

Rick Bass

A MARINER BOOK
HOUGHTON MIFFLIN COMPANY
Boston • New York

First Mariner Books edition 2007
Copyright © 2006 by Rick Bass
ALL RIGHTS RESERVED

www.houghtonmifflinbooks.com

Library of Congress Cataloging-in-Publication Data

Bass, Rick, date.
The lives of rocks : stories / Rick Bass.
p. cm.
ISBN-13: 978-0-618-59674-4
ISBN-10: 0-618-59674-7
I. Title.
PS3552.A8213L57 2006
813'.54 — dc22   2005037966

ISBN-13: 978-0-618-91966-6 (pbk.)
ISBN-10: 0-618-91966-X (pbk.)

Printed in the United States of America

Book design by Robert Overholtzer

MP 10 9 8 7 6 5 4 3 2 1

"Pagans," "The Canoeists," and "Goats" first appeared in the *Idaho Review.*
"Her First Elk" first appeared in the *Paris Review* and also in *Pushcart
Prize XXX.* "Yazoo" first appeared in the *Southern Review.* "The Lives of
Rocks" first appeared in *Zoetrope* and received the Texas Institute of Letters'
Kay Cattarulla/Brazos Bookstore Award for the short story. "Fiber" first
appeared in the *Mississippi Review.* "The Windy Day" first appeared in the
Quarterly. "Penetrations" first appeared in *Story,* and later, in slightly dif-
ferent form, in the *Seattle Review.* "Titan" first appeared in *Shenandoah.*

These stories are based on the imagination, and the characters in
them do not represent any persons known to me, living or not.

For Elizabeth, Mary Katherine, and Lowry,
and for Larry Brown

ACKNOWLEDGMENTS

I'M GRATEFUL to numerous editors for their help with these stories: as ever, my editor at Houghton Mifflin, Harry Foster, as well as Alison Kerr Miller and Reem Abu-Libdeh. I'm grateful also to editors who worked with these stories in earlier forms — George Plimpton, who is sorely missed, and the staff of the *Paris Review;* Michael Ray; Gordon Lish; Lois Rosenthal; and Rod Smith; and to the editors and staff of the *Seattle Review, Idaho Review, Mississippi Review,* and the *Southern Review,* as well. I'm grateful to Lynn Sainsbury; to my father for use of his old geology notes and texts; to my agent, Bob Dattila; to Russell Chatham for the beautiful painting on the cover; to the book's designer, Robert Overholtzer; to my typist, Angi Young; and to my family. I wish also to acknowledge the support and long friendship of the writer Larry Brown.

CONTENTS

The Lives of Rocks

PAGANS

THERE ONCE WERE two boys, best friends, who loved the same girl, and, in a less common variation on that ancient story, she chose neither of them but went on to meet and choose a third, and lived happily ever after.

One of the boys, Richard, nearly gambled his life on her — poured everything he had into the pursuit of her, Annie — while the other boy, Kirby, was attracted to her, intrigued by her, but not to the point where he would risk his life, or his heart, or anything else. It could have been said at the time that all three of them were fools, though no one who observed their strange courtship thought so, or said so; and even now, thirty years later, with the three of them as adrift and asunder from one another as any scattering of dust or wind, there are surely no regrets, no notions of failure or success or what-if, though among the three of them it is perhaps Richard alone who sometimes considers the past and imagines how easily things might have been different. How much labor went into the pursuit, and how close they, all three, passed to different worlds, different histories.

Richard and Kirby were seniors in high school while Annie was yet a junior, and as such they were able to get out of class easier than she was — they were both good students — and because Kirby had a car, an old Mercury with an engine like a locomotive's, he and Richard would sometimes spend their skip days traveling down to the coast, forty miles southeast of Houston, drawn by some force they neither understood nor questioned, traveling all the way to the water's lapping edge.

The boys traveled at night, too, always exploring, and on one of their trips they had found a rusting old crane half sunk near the estuary of the Sabine River, salt-bound, a derelict from gravel quarry days. They had climbed up into the crane (feeling like children playing in a sandbox) and found that they could manually unspool the loopy wire cable and with great effort crank it back in. (When they did so, the giant rusting gear teeth gave such a clacking roar that the night birds roosting down in the graystick spars of dead and dying trees on the other shore took flight, egrets and kingbirds and herons, the latter rising to fly long and slow and gangly across the moon; and as the flecks of rust chipped from each gear tooth during that groaning resurrection, the flakes drifted down toward the river in glittering red columns, fine as sand, orange wisps and strands of iron like magic dust being cast onto the river by the conjurings of some midnight sorcerer.)

With such power at their fingertips, there was no way not to exercise it. Richard climbed down from the crane and muck-waded out into the gray slime salt-rimmed shallows

— poisoned frogs yelped and skittered from his approach, and the orange sky-dancing flames of the nearby refineries wavered and belched, as if noticing his approach and beckoning him closer, as if desiring to stoke their own ceaseless burning with his own bellyfire.

Richard grabbed the massive hook of the cable's end and hauled it back up to shore and fastened it to the undercarriage of Kirby's car, then raised his hand over his head and made a twirling motion.

Kirby began cranking, and the car began to ascend in a levitation, rising slowly, easily, vertical into the air. Loose coins, pencils, and Coke cans tumbled from the windows at first, but then all was silent save for the steady ratchet of slow gears cranking one at a time, and the boys howled with pleasure, and more birds lifted from their rookeries and flew off uneasily into the night.

It was only when the car was some twenty feet in the air — dangling, bobbing, and spinning — that Richard thought to ask if the down gears worked, imagining what a long walk home it would be if they did not — and imagining, too, what the result might be if one of the old iron teeth failed, plummeting the Detroit beast into the mud below.

The gears held. Slowly, a foot at a time in its release, the crane let the car back down toward the road.

The boom would not pivot — had long ago been petrified into its one position, arching out toward the river like some tired monument facing the direction of a long-ago, all-but-forgotten war — but there were hundreds of feet of cable, so they were able to give each other rides in the rocket car now, one of them lifting it with the crane while the other gripped the steering wheel and held on for dear life, aiming straight for the moon and praying that the cable would hold.

They soon discovered that by twisting and jouncing around in the passenger seat they could induce the car to sway farther and even spin as it was raised — the Coriolis effect swirling below like an unseen, unmapped river — and it took all of an evening (the spinning headlights on high beam, strafing the mercury green bilious cloudbank above, where refinery steam crept through the tops of the trees) to tire of that game (startled birds flying right past the skydriver's windows, occasionally). They began hooking on to other objects, attaching the Great Claw of Hunger, as they called it, to anything substantial they could find: pulling from the sandbank half-submerged railroad ties, the old bumpers of junked cars, twisted steel scrap, rusting slag-heaped refrigerators, washers and dryers.

As if in a game of crude pinball or some remote-controlled claw clutch game at an arcade, they were able to lurch their attachments out into the center of the river; with a little practice, they learned how to disengage the hook in midair, which led to satisfying results — dropping junked cars into the river from forty feet up, landing them sometimes back on the road with a grinding clump of sparks, and other times in the river's center with a great whale plume of splash.

A sculpture soon appeared in the river's middle, a testament to machines that had been hard-used and burned out early, spring-busted not even halfway through the great century: the steel wheels of trains, cogs and pulleys, transmissions leaking rainbow sheens into the night water, iridescent sentences trailing slowly downstream in perhaps the same manner of the entrails that shamans once tossed to determine or sense world's flow and coming events. Within a few nights they had created an island in the slow current's middle, an island of steel and chrome that gathered the bask of reptiles on the hot days, and into the evenings — turtles, little alligators, snakes, and bullfrogs.

Nights were the best. There were still fireflies back then, along the Sabine, and the fireflies would cruise along the river and across the toxic fields, swirling around the angel-ascending car, the joy ride: and the riders, the journeyers, would imagine that they were astronauts, voyaging through the stars, cast out into some distant future.

In September the river was too low for barges to use, though when the rains of winter returned the river would rise quickly (flooding the banks and filling the cab of the crane), and the riverboat captains working at night would have to contend with the new obstacle of the junk slag island, not previously charted on their maps. They might or might not marvel at the origin or genesis of the structure, but would merely tug at the brims of their caps, note the obstacle in the logbook, and pass on, undreaming, laboring toward the lure of the ragged refineries, ferrying more oil and chemicals, hundreds of barrels of toxins sloshing quietly in the rusty steel drums stacked atop their barges, and never imagine that they were passing the fields of love . . .

Richard and Kirby bought an old diving bell in an army-navy surplus store for fifty dollars — they had to cut a new rubber gasket for the hatch's seal — and after that they were able to give each other crane rides into the poison river.

For each of them it was the same, whether lowering or being lowered: the crane's operator swinging the globe out over moonlit water the color of mercury, then lowering the globe, with his friend in it, into that netherworld — the passenger possessing only a flashlight, which dimmed quickly upon submersion and then disappeared — the globe tumbling with the current then and the passenger within not knowing whether or not the cable was still attached, bumping and tumbling, spotlight probing the black depths thinly, with brief, bright glimpses of fish eyes, gold-rimmed and wild in fright, and the pale turning-away bellies of wallowing things flashing past, darting left and right to get out of the way of the tumbling iron ball of the bathysphere.

The cable stretching taut, then, and shuddering against the relentless current: swaying and shimmering in place but traveling no more.

Then the emergence, back up out of total darkness and into the night. The gas flares still flickering all around them. Why, again, was the rest of the world asleep? The boys took comfort in the knowledge that they would never sleep: never.

On their afternoon school-skip trips together, the three of them traveling to the Gulf Coast, they would wander the beaches barefoot, walking beneath the strand line, studying the Gulf as if yearning to travel still farther — as if believing that, were they to catch it just right, the tide might one day pull back so far as to reveal the entire buried slope, wholly new territory — though this was not a clamant yearning, for already so much else was just as new. It was more like a consideration.

Beyond the smokestack flares of the refineries, out on a windy jetty, there was an abandoned lighthouse, its base barnacle-encrusted, that they enjoyed ascending on some such trips, and once up into the glassed-in cupola, they would drink hot chocolate from a thermos they had brought, sharing the one cup, and would play the board game Risk, to which they were addicted.

And, slowly, within Annie, a little green fire began to burn as she spent more and more time with the two older boys;

and, more quickly, an orange fire began to flicker, then burn within Richard as he began to desire to spend more and more time in her company.

Only Kirby seemed immune, his own internal light cool and blue.

They played on.

By mid-September Kirby and Richard were bringing Annie out to play the bathysphere game, and to view their slag island. They would come out on lunch break, and would skip a class before and sometimes after to buy them the time they needed. There was a bohemian French-African oceanography teacher who was retiring that year and who could see plainly what Richard, if not Kirby, was trying to do, chasing the heart of the young girl, the junior. The teacher — Miss Counteé, who wore a beret — would write hall passes for all three of them, knowing full well that they would be leaving campus, issuing the passes under the stipulation that they bring back specimens for her oceanography lab. They drove through the early autumn heat with the windows down and an old green canoe on top of their car. They paddled out to the new slag island and had picnics of French bread and green apples and cheese.

They piled lawn chairs atop the edifice. And even though the water was poisoned, the sound of it, as they lay there in the sun with their sleeves rolled up and their shoes and socks off, eyes closed, was the same as would be the sound of waves in the Bahamas, or a clear cold stream high in the mountains. Just because the water was ugly did not mean it had to sound ugly.

Richard knew that to the rest of the world Annie might have appeared slightly gangly, even awkward, but that had nothing to do with how his heart leapt now each time he saw her — and after they began traveling to the river, he started to notice new things about her. Her feet pale in the sun, her shoulders rounding, her breasts lifting. A softening in her eyes as the beauty in her heart began to rise out of her. And many years later, after their lives separated, he would believe that there was something about the sound, the harmonics, of that ravaged river and her ability to love it, and take pleasure in it, that released something from within her: transforming in ancient alchemy the beautiful unseen into the beautifully tangible.

The water lapping lightly against the edges of the green canoe, tethered to one of the steel spars midpile. Umbrellas for parasols: crackers and cheese. Annie's pale feet browning in the sun. Perspiration at their temples, under their arms, in the small of their backs. Richard felt himself descending, sinking deeper into love, or what he supposed was love. How many years, he wondered, before the two of them were married and they would browse upon each other, in similar sunlight, in another country, another life? He was content to wait forever.

It was, however, as if Annie's own fire, the quiet green one, would not or could not quite merge with his leaping, dancing orange one. As if the two fires (or three fires) needed to be in each other's company and were supported, even fed, by each other's warmth — but that they could not, or would not yet, combine.

Without true heat of conviction, Annie would sometimes try to view the two boys separately, and would even, in her girl's way, play or pretend at imagining a future. Kirby, she told herself, was more mature, more responsible — he could run an old crane! As well, there was an instinct that seemed to counsel her to both be drawn toward yet also move away from Richard's own more exposed fires and energies.

It was too much work to consider; it was all pretend anyway, or almost pretend. They had found a lazy place, a sweet place, to hang out, in the eddy between childhood and whatever came next. She told herself that she would be happy to wait there forever, and, for a while, she believed that.

Occasionally, the befouled river would ignite spontaneously; other times, they found that they could light it themselves by tossing matches or flaming oily rags out onto its oil and chemical slicks. None of the three of them was a church-goer, though Annie, a voracious reader, had been carrying around a Bible that autumn, reading it silently on their picnics while crunching an apple. The bayou breeze, river breeze, stirring her strawberry hair.

"I want to give the river a blessing," she said the first time she saw the river ignite. The snaky, wandering river fires, in various bright petrochemical colors, seemed more like a celebration than a harbinger of death or poison, and they told themselves that through such incinerations they were doing the river a favor, helping to rid it of excess toxins.

They loaded their green canoe with gallon jugs of water the next day, tap water straight from their Houston faucets and hoses.

The canoe rode low in the poisoned water on their short trip out to the iron-and-chrome island, carrying the load of the three of them as well as their jugs of water. The gunwales of their green boat were no more than an inch above the vile murk of the river, and they sat in the canoe as still as perched birds to avoid capsizing, letting the current carry them to the island of trash.

Once there, they spent nearly the rest of the afternoon scrubbing with steel wool and pouring the clean bright water over the crusted, rusted, mud-slimed ornamenture of bumpers and freezers, boat hulls and car bodies. They polished the chrome appurtenances and rinsed the mountain anew. They waded around its edges, oblivious to the sponges of their own pure skin taking in the river's, and the world's, poison.

When they had it sparkling, Annie climbed barefoot to the top and read a quote from Jeremiah: "And I brought you into the plentiful country, to eat the fruit thereof and the goodness thereof; but when ye entered, ye defiled my land and made mine heritage an abomination."

On her climb up to the top, she had gashed her foot on the rusted corner of one sharp piece or another. She paid it no mind as she stood up there in her overalls, her red-brown hair stirring in the wind, a startlingly bright trickle of blood leaking from her pale foot, and Richard had the uneasy feeling that something whole and vital and time-crafted, rare and pure, was leaking out of her through that wound, and that he — with his strange vision of the world and his half-assed, dreamy shenanigans — was partly responsible: if not for leading her directly astray, then at least for leading her down the path to the flimsy or even unlatched gate, and showing her a view beyond.

And Kirby, too, viewing her blood, felt an almost overpowering wave of tenderness, and with his bare hand quickly wiped the blood from her foot, then put his arm around her as if to comfort her, though she did not feel discomforted:

and now the two of them sank a bit deeper into the fields of love, like twin pistons dropping a little deeper, leaving Richard off-balance for a moment, for a day, poised above, distanced now . . .

There was no clean water left with which to rinse or purify themselves after the ceremony. Instead they burned handfuls of green Johnson grass, wands of slow-swirling blue smoke. Like pagans, they paddled back to shore, mucked across the oily sandbar, and while Richard and Kirby were loading the canoe back onto the car, Annie went off into the tall waving grass to pee, and when she came back she was carrying a dead white egret: not one of the splendid but common yellow-legged cattle egrets but a larger and much rarer snowy egret (within their lifetime it would all but vanish), whiter than even the clouds — so white that as Annie carried it it seemed to glow. And it had died so recently that it was still limp.

She laid it down in the grass for them to examine. They stroked its head, and the long crested plumes flowing from the head. Perhaps it was only sleeping. Perhaps they could resuscitate it. Kirby stretched the wings out into a flying position, then folded them back in tight against the body. Nothing. Annie's eyes watered, and again Kirby felt the overpowering wave of tenderness that was not brotherly but stronger, wilder, fiercer: as if it came from the river itself.

It seemed that the obvious thing to do would be to bury the egret, but they couldn't bring themselves to give such beauty back to the earth, much less to such an oily, drippy, poisoned earth, and so they took the canoe and paddled back out to the island and laid the bird — fierce-eyed and thick-beaked — to rest in the crown of the island, staring downriver like a gunner in his turret, with the breeze stirring his elegant plumage and a wreath of green grass in a garland around his snowy neck.

This time on the way out they remembered their oceanography assignment and scooped up a mayonnaise jar full of water and sediment that was the approximate color and consistency of watery diarrhea, and swabbed a dip net through the grass shallows, coming up with a quick catch of crabs and bent-backed, betumored mullet minnows. Then they loaded the canoe and drove back to school through the brilliant heat, the brilliant light, the three of them riding in the front seat together.

When they got back to school — a feeling like checking back into a jail — they hurried up the stairwell with their fetid bounty, late to class as usual, and placed their murky-watered bottles on the cool marble lab table at the front of the room for the rest of the class to see.

Miss Counteé made alternating clucking sounds of pleasure and then dismay as she examined the macroinvertebrates as well as the crippled vertebrates, murmuring their names in genus and species, not as if naming them but as if greeting old acquaintances, old warriors, perhaps, from another time and place — and the other students got up from their seats and crowded around the jars and bottles as if to be closer to the presence of magic.

Richard and Annie and Kirby would still have the marsh scent of the river on them, and the blue smoke odor of burnt Johnson grass, and sometimes, for a moment, Miss Counteé and the students would get the strange feeling that the true wildness was not the catch in the mayonnaise jars but the catchers themselves.

Miss Counteé took an eyedropper and drew up a shot of dead Sabine, dripped it onto a slide, slid it under a microscope, and then crooned at all the violent erratica dashing about beneath her: the athleticism and diversity, the starts and stops and lunges, the silky passages, the creepings and slitherings, the throbbings and pulsings.

The river was dying, but it was still alive.

By October the leaves on the wounded trees at water's edge were turning yellow, and Annie was riding in the bathysphere.

As the sphere tumbled, she could orient herself to the surface by the bright glare above — the bouncy, jarring ride to the bottom, the tumultuous drift downstream, and then the shuddering tautness when the cable reached full draw. Usually she was busy laughing or praying for her life, but sometimes, at full stretch, she considered sex.

The crane lifted the sphere free and clear of the river: back into that bright light, water cascading off the bathysphere and glittering in sheets and torrents of sun diamonds (the awful river transformed, in that moment, into something briefly beautiful). Sometimes, to tease her, the boys would let her remain down there just a beat or two longer, each time: just long enough for the precursor of a thought to begin to enter her mind, the image that — despite their obvious affection for her — something had snapped within them. Not quite the thought, but the advancing shadow of the thought — the chemical synapses stirring and shifting, rearranging themselves to accommodate the approaching, imagined conception — of the boys, her friends, climbing down from the crane and getting in the car and driving off.

Not *abandoning* her, but going off for a burger and fries. And then forgetting her, perhaps, or getting in a wreck.

Always, the boys pulled her up and reeled her back in before the thought of abandonment came, and the thought beyond that — the terror of utter loneliness, utter emptiness.

None of them questioned that the crane was there for them, a relic still operating for them. They didn't question that it was tucked out of the way below a series of dunes and bluffs, away from the prying, curious eyes of man, and didn't question the grace, the luck, that allowed them to run it, day or night, unobserved. They didn't question that the world, the whole world, belonged to them.

There were still a million, or maybe a hundred thousand, or at least ten thousand such places left in the world back then. Soft seams of possibility, places where no boundaries had been claimed — places where reservoirs of infinite potential lay exposed and waiting for the claimant, the discoverer, the laborer, the imaginer. Places of richness and health, even in the midst of heart-rotting, gut-eating poisons.

For the first time, however, Richard and Kirby began to view each other as competitors. It was never a thought that lasted; always, they were ashamed of it and able to banish it at will: but for the first time, it was there.

The egret fell to pieces slowly. Sun-baked, rained-upon, wind-ruffled, ant-eaten, it deflated as if only now was its life leaving it; and then it disintegrated further until soon there were only piles of sun-bleached feathers lying in the cracks and crevices of the junk-slag island below, and feathers loose, too, within the ghost frame of its own skeleton, still up there at the top of the machines.

As the egret decomposed, so too was revealed the quarry within — the last meal upon which it had gorged — and they could see within the bone basket of its rib cage all the tiny fish skeletons, with their piles of scale glitter lying around like bright sand. There were bumps and tumors, misshapen bends in the fishes' skeletons, and as they rotted (flies feasting on them within that ventilated rib cage, as if trapped in a bottle, but free, also, to come and go) the toxic sludge of their lives melted to leave a bright metallic residue on the island, staining here and there like stripes of silver paint.

Sometimes they would be too restless to fool with even the magnificence of the crane. Bored with the familiar, the three of them would walk down the abandoned railroad tracks, gathering plump late-season dewberries, blackening their hands with the juice until they looked as if they had been working with oil. Kirby or Richard would take off his shirt and make a sling out of it in which to gather the berries. Their mouths, their lips, would be black-ringed, like clowns'.

She beheld their bodies. They filled her dreams — first one boy, then the other — as did dreams of ghost ships, and underworld rides. Dreams of a world surely different from this one — a fleshing, a stripping back to reveal the bones and flesh, the red muscle of a world not at all like the image of the one we believe we have crafted above.

Unsettling dreams, to be shaken off, with difficulty, upon awakening. Surely all below is only imagined, she tried to tell herself, only fantasy. Surely there is only one world.

The berries they brought home were sweet and delicious, ripe and plump. The dreams of gas flares and simmering underworld fires, only images, possessed nothing of the berries' reality. Only one world, she told herself. There is nothing to be frightened of, no need to be cautious about anything.

The cracks and fissures of chance, the ruptures at the earth's surface claiming the three of them, then, as surely as all must be claimed — those crevices, crevasses, manifesting or masquerading as random occurrence rather than design or pattern but operating surely, just beneath the surface, in intricate balancings of need-and-desire, cost-and-recompense — an alignment of fates as crafted and organic, almost always, as the movements of the tides themselves. There was a school Halloween dance that autumn, a party, which Kirby was unable to attend due to some family matter that had arisen just that week. The crack or crevice, seemingly without meaning.

It was a low-key evening filled with chaperones, and with the elementary and middle schools combining, that evening, with the high schoolers. The party was filled with Twister and pin the tail on the donkey and Bingo and bobbing for apples. There was a haunted house, and masked children of all ages in all manners of costumes ran laughing and shouting through the school hallways, and the high schoolers hung back for a while but then gave themselves over to the fun.

There was dancing in the basketball gym, with some of the children and adults still wearing their masks and costumes, though many of the teenagers had taken off their masks and were now only half animal — tiger, fairy, princess, gorilla. Their faces were flushed, and the discrepancy between what their hormones were telling them — *destroy, rebel* — and what the rigid bars of their culture were telling them — *no, no, no* — was for the most lively of them like a pressure cooker.

Annie was dressed as a princess, and Richard a red devil. They sat for a while and watched the other children dance. Annie waited and was aware of no pressure. It's possible that she could afford to step aside of the drumming, mounting pressure her peers were feeling because most days she had Richard and Kirby in her life, and Richard at her side, much as a young girl might have a pet bear or lion in her backyard. She turned and smiled at Richard, serene, while the records played and the little monsters ran shrieking, bumping against their legs. The scent of sugar in the air. Around them the dense aura of all the other itchy, troubled, angst-bound teenagers, wanting sex, wanting power, wanting God, wanting salvation — wanting home and hearth, and yet also wanting the open road.

There was no need yet for Annie to participate in any of that confusion. Everything else around her was swirling and tattering, but she was grounded and centered, and she was loved deeply, without reason. She smiled, watching Richard watch the dancers. She reached over and took his hand in the darkness and held it, while they watched, and as they felt the palpable fretting and shifting of their peers. It was lonely, being sunk down to the bottom of the world, she thought, but comfortable, even wonderful, to have each other during such a journey.

"What do you think Kirby's doing right now?" she asked, twisting his hand in hers.

They left the party and went out for an ice cream sundae and enjoyed it leisurely, watching the rest of the city zoom by out on the neon strip of Westheimer Road, a busy Friday night, hearing dimly even in the restaurant the whooping and shouting from open car windows and the screeching of tires, and gears accelerating.

They enjoyed the meal with no conscious forethought of where they were going next — though if anyone had asked them, they would have been able to answer immediately, and after a little while Kirby drove past, finished with his family engagement. He saw Richard's car, and pulled in and joined them.

With Richard and Annie still wearing their costumes, they journeyed east, riding with the windows down as ever, and with the radio playing, but with a seriousness, a quietness, the three of them knowing with adults' wisdom that they were ascending now into the world ahead, as if to some upper level, a level that would sometimes be exciting but where more frequent work would be the order of the day: less dreaming and more awareness and consciousness. Carve and scribe, hammer and haul. Almost like a war. As if this unasked-for war must be, and was, the price of all their earlier peace, and all their peace to come.

Richard and Annie held hands again in the car on the way east, and the three of them knew by the way the crane's allure was dying within them as they drew nearer to that sulfurous, wavering glow on the horizon that they would soon be moving on to other things, and in other directions. It was almost as if now — for the first time — they were pushing into a heavy headwind.

It was getting late. The city's children had finished their trick-or-treating. As they passed through a small wooded suburb sandwiched between shopping malls, they stopped and went up and gathered several stubbed candle remnants from the scorched mouths of sagging, sinking, barely glimmering pumpkins.

One pumpkin had already been taken out to the sidewalk for the garbage men to pick up the next morning, and they resurrected that one, placed it on the front seat between Annie and Kirby, and fed it a new candle, coaxing it back to brightness as one might offer a cigarette to an injured or dying soldier.

They rode through the city and then east toward the refineries, with their runty candles wax-welded all over the front and back dashboards, the windows rolled almost all the way up now to keep from extinguishing the little flames — the light on their faces wavering as they passed through the night (to the passengers in the passing cars and trucks, it seemed strangely as if Kirby and Richard and Annie were floating, so disorienting was the sight of the big car filled with all those candles — and they kept heading east, toward the flutterings and spumes of the refineries' chemical fires, toward that strange glow that was like daytime at night.

That night Annie and Richard went down into the bathysphere, and into the river, together, with Kirby above them, working the manual crank on the crane like a puppeteer. They were still wearing their costumes — there was barely room for them to squeeze in together, and Annie's satin dress spread across the whole bench, and Richard's devil's tail got folded beneath them — he rode with his arm around her, and hers around him, for stability as well as courage, as the globe was lifted, swaying, from the earth — that first familiar and sickening feeling of powerlessness as the ground fell away below them — and they rode with an array of candles in front of them.

Their faces were almost touching. *This,* Richard was thinking, *this is how I want it always to be.*

They glimpsed the stars, swinging, as Kirby levered them out over the river, and then there was the thrill of free fall — "Hold on!" Richard shouted, covering her with both arms and shielding her head — and the concussion of iron meeting water, the great splash — candles went everywhere, spilling warm wax on their hands and wrists, their faces — one landed on Annie's dress and burned a small hole into it — and then, once underwater, the globe righted itself and settled in for the brief ride downstream. With the candles that were still burning they relit the scattered ones and leaned forward, and cheek to cheek they studied the interior of the foul river as they tumbled slowly through its center.

"What if the cable snapped loose," Richard asked, "when we hit the water so hard?"

Not to be outdone, Annie said, "What if some old bum, as a Halloween joke, sawed the cable down to its last fiber, so that when we reach the end it will snap?"

There was a long silence as Richard's imagination seized and worked with that one for a while, until it became too true, and he sought to change the outcome.

"What if we were stranded on a desert island?" Richard asked.

"How about a forested island?"

"Right," Richard said. "What if? And what if we had only a little while to live?"

"The last man and woman on earth," Annie said.

"Right." *Man and woman.* The phrase sounded so foreign and distant: light-years away, still.

"Well," said Annie, "let's wait and see." But her arm tight-ened around his significantly, and Richard found himself urging the cable to *break, break, break.*

The cable reached full stretch; there was a bumping, and then the globe was swept up and out, tumbling them onto their backs — as if a carpet had been pulled from beneath their feet — and again the candles fell over on them, as did the hot wax, and this time no candles stayed lit, so that they shuddered in darkness, feeling the waves, the intimate urgings of the injured river, washing over and around their tiny iron shell.

The force of the current made eerie sounds, murmurings and chatterings against their craft, as if it, that sick river, had been waiting to speak to them for all their life and had only now gained that opportunity — and they lay there, reclining in each other's arms, safe from the eyes of the world and its demands, its appetites for paradox and choice; and just as the air was beginning to get stuffy and they were beginning to get a little lightheaded, they felt the surge begin: the mag-nificent power, the brute imprecision of gears and cogs haul-ing them back upstream, just when they would have imag-ined (convinced by those fast murmurings and chatterings) that there could be no force stronger or greater than that of the river.

Gradually they broke the surface — through their portal, still lying on their backs and arm in arm, but relaxed now, they could see the plumes and spray of water as they were birthed back to the surface; they could see the crooked, jar-ring skyline of the refinery fires, and farther above the dim stars just beyond the reach of the gold-green luminous puffs of steam that marked the factories.

There was not much time now. Soon they would be up and free of the river, swinging, and then Kirby would land them on the beach. They were hot now, sweating, and there was barely any air left. Annie leaned over and found Richard's face with her hands, and kissed him slowly, with both hands still on his face. He kissed her back — took her face in his hands and tried to shift in order to cover her with his body, but there was no room — for a moment, they became tangled, cross-elbowed and leg-locked like some human Rubik's cube. They broke off the kiss quickly, and now there was no air at all — as if they had each sucked the last of it from out of the other — but they could feel the craft settling onto the sand beach now and knew that in scant moments Kirby would be climbing down and coming toward them, that there would be the rap of his knuckles on the iron door, and then the creak of the hatch being opened.

Time for one more kiss, demure and tender now, and then the gritty rasp of the hatch: the counterclockwise twist, and then the lid being lifted, and Kirby's anxious face appearing before them, and beyond him, those dim stars, almost like the echoes or spent husks of stars. Cool October night sliding in over their sweaty faces.

Richard helped Annie out — her dress was a charred mess — and then climbed out behind her, marveling at how delicious even the foul refinery air tasted in their freedom. Kirby looked at them both curiously and started to speak, but then could think of nothing to say, and he felt a strange and great sorrow.

They left the bathysphere as it was, sitting with the hatch opened, still attached to the crane with its steel umbilicus; for any number of reasons, none of them would ever go back; they would never see how the crane would eventually tip over on its side, half buried in silt, or how the bathy-sphere would become buried, too.

They rode back into the city, still in costume, silent and strangely serious, reflective on the trip home, and with the pumpkin and candles glimmering once more, and with Annie and Richard holding hands again. The candle wax was still on their faces, and it looked molten upon them in the candlelight.

On the drive home Annie peeled the candle wax from her face and then from Richard's, and she held the pressings carefully in one hand.

When Kirby pulled up in front of her house — the living room lights still on, and one of them, mother or father, wait-ing up, and glancing at the clock (ten minutes past eleven, but no matter; they trusted her) — Annie leaned over and gave Richard a quick peck, and gave Kirby a look of almost sultry forgiveness, then climbed out of the big old car (they had extinguished their candles upon entering the neighbor-hood) and hurried up the walkway to her house, holding her long silk skirt bunched up in one hand and the candle wax pressings in another.

"Well, *fuck*," said Kirby, quietly, unsure of whether he was more upset about what seemed to him like Annie's sudden choice or about the fracturing that now existed between him and his friend. The imbalance, after so long a run, an all-but-promised run, of security.

"Shit," said Richard, "I'm sorry." He lifted his hands help-lessly. "Can we . . . can it . . . ?" *Stay the same*, he wanted to say, but didn't.

They both sat there, feeling poisoned, even as the other half of Richard's heart — as if hidden behind a mask — was leaping with electric joy.

"I'm sorry," Richard said again.

"The two of you deserve each other," Kirby said. "It's just that, I hate it that . . ." But the words failed him; there were none, only the bad burning feeling within, and after sitting there awhile longer, they pulled away from her house and drove for a while through the night, as they used to do, back before she had begun riding with them. And for a little while they were foolish enough, and hopeful enough, to believe that it would not matter, that they could get back to that old place again, and even that that old place would be finer than any new places lying ahead of them.

The romance lasted only a little longer than did the carcass of the egret. The three of them continued to try to do new things together — they did not return to the bathysphere — though Richard and Annie went places by themselves, too, and explored, tentatively, those new territories. Always between or beneath them, however, there seemed to be a burr: not that she had made the wrong choice, but rather that some choice had been required — that she had had to turn away from one thing even in the turning-toward another — and that summer, even before the two boys, two young men, prepared to go off to college, while Annie readied herself to return for her senior year of high school, she informed Richard that she thought she would like a couple of weeks apart to think things over and to prepare for the pain of his departure. To prepare both of them.

"My God," Richard said, "*two* weeks?" They had been seeing each other almost every day. Their bodies had changed, their voices had changed, as had their patterns and gestures, and even the shapes of their faces, becoming leaner and more adultlike, so that now when Annie placed the old wax pressings to her face, they no longer fit.

"I want to see what it's like," she said. "Maybe everything will be just fine. Maybe we'll find out we can't live without each other, and we'll end up married and raising children and happy ever after. But I just want to know."

"All right," he said, far more frightened than he'd ever been while dangling from the crane. "All right," he said, and it seemed to him that it was as if she were climbing into the bathysphere alone, and he marveled at her bravery and curiosity, her adventurousness, and even her wisdom.

There is still a sweetness in all three of their lives now: Kirby, with his wife and four children, in a small town north of Houston; Richard, with his wife and two children; and Annie, with her husband and five children, and, already, her first grandchild. A reservoir of sweetness, a vast subterranean vault of it, like the treasure lair of savages — the past, hidden far away in their hearts, and held, and treasured, mythic and powerful, even now.

It was exactly like the treasure-trove of wild savages, they each realize now, and for some reason — grace? simple luck? — they were able to dip down into it back then, were able to scrape out handfuls of it, gobs of it, like sugar or honey.

As if it — the discovery of that reservoir — remains with them, a power and a strength, so many years later.

And yet — they had all once been together. How can they now be apart, particularly if that reservoir remains intact, buried, and ever-replenishing?

Even now, Richard thinks they missed each other by a hair's breadth, that some sort of fate was deflected — though how or why or what, he cannot say. He thinks it might have been one of the closest misses in the history of the world. He has no regrets, only marvels. He wonders sometimes if there are not the ghosts or husks of their other lives living still, far back in the past, or far below, or even farther out into the future: still together, and still consorting; other lives, birthed from that strange reservoir of joy and sweetness, and utter newness.

And if there are, how does he access that? Through memory? Through imagination?

Even now, he marvels at how wise they were then, and at all the paths they did not take.

HER FIRST ELK

SHE HAD KILLED an elk once. She had been a young woman, just out of college — her beloved father already three years in the grave — and had set out early on opening morning, hiking uphill through a forest of huge ponderosa pines, with the stars shining like sparks through their boughs, and owls calling all around her, and her breath rising strong in puffs and clouds as she climbed, and a shimmering at the edge of her vision like the electricity in the night sky that sometimes precedes the arrival of the northern lights, or heat lightning.

The hunt was over astonishingly quickly; years later, she would realize that the best hunts stretch out four or five weeks, and sometimes never result in a taking. But this one had ended in the first hour, on the first day.

Even before daylight, she had caught the scent of the herd bedded down just ahead of her, a scent sweeter and ranker than that of any number of stabled horses; and creeping closer, she had been able to hear their herd sounds, their little mewings and grunts.

She crouched behind one of the giant trees, shivering from both the cold and her excitement — sharply, she had the thought that she wished her father were there with her, that one morning, to see this, to participate — and then she was shivering again, and there was nothing in her mind but elk.

Slowly, the day became light, and she sank lower into the tall grass beneath the big pines, the scent of the grass sweet upon her skin; and the lighter the day became, the farther she flattened herself down into that yellow grass.

The elk rose to their feet just ahead of her, and at first she thought they had somehow scented her, even though the day's warming currents had not yet begun to ascend the hill — even though the last of the night's heavier, cooling currents were still sliding in rolling waves down the mountain, the faint breeze in her face carrying the ripe scent of the herd downhill, straight to her.

But they were only grazing, wandering around now, still mewing and clucking and barking and coughing, and feeding on the same sweet-scented grass that she was hiding in. She could hear their teeth grinding as they chewed, could hear the clicking of their hoofs as they brushed against rocks.

These creatures seemed a long way from the dinners that her father had fixed out on the barbecue grill, bringing in the sizzling red meat and carving it quickly before putting it on her child's plate and saying, "Elk"; but it was the same animal — they were all the same animal, nearly a dozen years later. Now the herd was drifting like water, or slow-flickering flames, out of the giant pines and into a stand of aspen, the gold leaves underfoot the color of their hides, and the stark white trunks of the aspen grove making it look as if the herd were trapped behind bars; though still they kept drifting, flowing in and out of and between those bars, and when Jyl saw the biggest one, the giant among them, she picked him, not knowing any better — unaware that the meat would be tougher than that of a younger animal. Raising up on one knee, she found the shot no more difficult for her than sinking a pool ball in a corner pocket: tracking with the end of her rifle and the crosshairs of the scope, the cleft formed just behind his right shoulder as he quartered away from her, she did not allow herself to be distracted by the magnificent crown of antlers atop his head — and when he stopped, in his last moment, and swung his head to face her, having sensed her presence, she squeezed the trigger as she had been taught to do back when she was a girl. The giant elk leapt hump-shouldered like a bull in a rodeo, then took a few running steps before stumbling, as if the bullet had not shredded his heart and half his lungs but had instead merely confused him.

He crashed heavily to the ground, as if attached to an invisible tether; got up, ran once more, and fell again.

The cows and calves in his herd, as well as the younger bulls, stared at him, trying to discern his meaning, and disoriented, too, by the sudden explosive sound. They stared at the source of the sound — Jyl had risen to her feet and was watching the great bull's thrashings, wondering whether to shoot again, and still the rest of the herd stared at her with what she could recognize only as disbelief.

The bull got up and ran again. This time he did not fall, having figured out, in his grounded thrashings, how to accommodate his strange new dysfunction so as to not impede his desire, which was to escape — and with one leg and shoulder tucked high against his chest, like a man carrying a satchel, and his hind legs spread wider for stability, he galloped off, running now like a horse in hobbles and with his immense mahogany-colored rack tipped back for balance: what was once his pride and power was now a liability.

The rest of the herd turned and followed him into the timber, disappearing into the forest's embrace almost reluctantly, still possessing somehow that air of disbelief; though once they went into the timber, they vanished completely, and for a long while she could hear the crashing of limbs and branches — as if she had unleashed an earthquake or some other world force — and the sounds grew fainter and farther, and then there was only silence.

Not knowing any better, back then, she set out after the herd rather than waiting to let the bull settle down and lie down and bleed to death. She didn't know that if pushed a bull could run for miles with his heart in tatters, running as if on magic or spirit rather than the conventional pump-house mechanics of ventricles and aortas; that if pushed, a bull could run for months with his lungs exploded or full of blood. As if in his dying the bull were able to metamorphose into some entirely other creature, taking its air, its oxygen, straight into its blood, through its gaping, flopping mouth, as a fish does; and as if it were able still to disseminate and retrieve its blood, pressing and pulsing it to the farthest reaches of its body and back again without the use of a heart, relying instead on some kind of mysterious currents and desire — the will to cohere — far larger than its own, the blood sloshing back and forth, back and forth, willing the elk forward, willing the elk to keep being an elk.

Jyl had had it in her mind to go to the spot where the elk

had first fallen — even from where she was, fifty or sixty yards distant, she could see the patch of torn-up earth — and to find the trail of blood from that point, and to follow it.

She was already thinking ahead, and looking beyond that first spot — having not yet reached it — when she walked into the barbed-wire fence that separated the national forest from the adjoining private property, posted against hunting, on which the big herd had been sequestered.

The fence was strung so tight that she bounced backwards, falling much as the elk had fallen, that first time; and in her inexperience, she had been holding the trigger on her rifle, with a shell chambered in case she should see the big bull again, and as she fell she gripped the trigger, discharging the rifle a second time, with a sound even more cavernous, in its unexpectedness, than the first shot.

A branch high above her intercepted the bullet, and the limb came floating slowly down, drifting like a kite. From her back, she watched it land quietly, and she continued to lie there, bleeding a little, and trembling, before finally rising and climbing over the fence, with its "Posted" signs, and continuing on after the elk.

She was surprised by how hard it was to follow his blood trail: only a damp splatter here and there, sometimes red and other times drying brown already against the yellow aspen leaves that looked like spilled coins — as if some thief had been wounded while ferrying away a strongbox and had spilled his blood upon that treasure.

She tried to focus on the task at hand but was aware also of feeling strangely and exceedingly lonely — remembering, seemingly from nowhere, that her father had been red-green colorblind, and realizing how difficult it might have been for him to see those drops of blood. Wishing again that he were here with her, though, to help her with the tracking of this animal.

It was amazing to her how little blood there was. The entry wound, she knew, was no larger than a straw, and the exit wound wouldn't be much larger than a quarter, and even that small wound would be partially closed up with the shredded flesh, so that almost all of the blood would still be inside the animal, sloshing around, hot and poisoned now, no longer of use but unable to come out.

A drop here, a drop there. She couldn't stop marveling at how few clues there were. It was easier to follow the tracks in the soft earth, and the swath of broken branches, than it was the blood trail — though whether she was following the herd's path or the bull's separate path, she couldn't be entirely sure.

She came to the edge of the timber and looked out across a small plowed field, the earth dark from having just been turned over to autumn stubble. Her elk was collapsed dead out in the middle of it — the rest of the herd was long gone, nowhere to be seen — and there was a truck parked next to the elk already, and standing next to the elk were two older men in cowboy hats. Jyl was surprised, then, at how tall the antlers were — taller than either man, even with the elk lying stretched out on the bare ground; taller even than the cab of the truck.

The men did not appear happy to see her coming. It seemed to take her a long time to reach them, and it was hard walking over the furrows and clods of stubble, and from the looks on the men's faces, she was afraid that the elk might have been one of their pets, that they might even have given it a name.

It wasn't that bad, as it turned out, but it still wasn't good. Their features softened a little as she closed the final distance and they saw how young she was, and how frightened — she could have been either man's daughter — and as she approached there seemed to be some force of energy about her that disposed them to think the best of her; they found it hard to believe, too, that had she killed the elk illegally she would be marching right up to claim it.

There were no handshakes, no introductions. There was still frost on the windshield of the men's truck, and Jyl realized they must have jumped into their truck and cold-started it, racing straight up to where they knew the herd hung out. Used to hang out.

Plumes of fog-breath leapt from the first man's mouth as he spoke, even though they were all three standing in the sunlight.

"You shot it over on the other side of the fence, right, over on the national forest, and it leapt the fence and came over here to die?" he asked, and he was not being sarcastic: as if, now that he could see Jyl's features, and her fear and youth, he could not bear to think of her as a poacher.

The other man, who appeared to be a few years the elder — they looked like brothers, with the older one somewhere in his sixties, and fiercer-looking — interrupted before she could answer and said, "Those elk knew never to cross that fence during hunting season. That bull wouldn't let them. I've been watching him for five years, and any time a cow or calf even *looks* at that fence, he tips — tipped — his antlers at them and herded them away from it."

Jyl saw that such an outburst was as close to a declaration of love for the animal as the old man would be capable of uttering, and the three of them looked down at the massive animal, whose body heat they could still feel radiating from it — the twin antlers larger than any swords of myth, and the elk's eyes closed, and still only what seemed like a little blood dribbling down the left shoulder, from the exit wound — the post-rut musk odor of the bull was intense — and all Jyl could say was "I'm sorry."

The younger brother seemed almost alarmed by this admission.

"You didn't shoot him on our side, did you?" he asked again. "For whatever reason — maybe a cow or calf had hopped the fence, and he was over there trying to get it back into the herd — he was over on the public land, and you shot him, and he ran back this way, jumped over the fence, and ran back over here, right?"

Jyl looked down at her feet, and then again at the bull. She might as well have shot an elephant, she thought. She felt trembly, nauseated. She glanced at her rifle to be sure the chamber was open.

"No," she said quietly.

"Oh, Christ," the younger man said — the older one just glared at her, hawkish, but also slightly surprised now — and again the younger one said, "Are you sure? Maybe you didn't see it leap the fence?"

Jyl showed him the scratch marks on her arms, and on her face. "I didn't know the fence was there," she said. "The sun was coming up and I didn't see it. After I shot, I walked into the fence."

Both men stared at her as if she were some kind of foreigner, or as if she were making some fabulous claim and challenging them to believe it.

"What was the second shot?" the older man asked, looking

back toward the woods. "Why did it come so much later?" As if suspecting that she might have a second animal down somewhere, back in the forest. As if this frail girl, this *child*, might have a vendetta against the herd.

"The gun went off by accident, when I walked into the fence," she said, and both men frowned in a way that told her that gun carelessness was even worse in their book than elk poaching.

"Is it unloaded now?" the younger brother asked, almost gently.

"No," she said, "I don't guess it is."

"Why don't you unload it now?" he asked, and she complied, bolting and unbolting the magazine three times, with a gold cartridge cartwheeling to the black dirt each time, and then a fourth time, different-sounding, less full sounding, snicking the magazine empty. She felt a bit of tension release from both men, and in some strange way of the hunt that she had not yet learned, the elk seemed somehow different, too: less vital, in her letting-down. As if, despite its considerable power and vitality, her pursuit of and hunger for it had somehow helped to imbue it with even more of those characteristics, sharpening their edges, if only just a little.

The older brother crouched down and picked up the three cartridges and handed them to her. "Well, goddamn," he said, after she had put them in her pocket and stood waiting for him to speak — would she go to jail? would she be arrested, or fined? — "That's a big animal. I don't suppose you have much experience cleaning them, do you?"

She shook her head.

The brothers looked back down the hill — in the direction of their farmhouse, Jyl supposed. The fire unstoked, the breakfast unmade. Autumn chores still undone, with snow coming any day and a whole year's worth of battening down, or so it seemed, to do in that narrow wedge of time.

"Well, let's do it right," the elder said. "Come with us back down to the house and we'll get some warm water and towels, a saw and ax and a come-along." He squinted at her, more curious than unkind. "What did you intend to do, after shooting this animal?" he asked.

Jyl patted her hip. "I've got a pocketknife," she said. Both brothers looked at each other and then broke into incredulous laughter, with tears coming to the eyes of the younger one.

"Might I see it?" the younger one asked when he could catch his breath, but the querulous civility of his question set his brother off to laughing again — they both broke into guffaws — and when Jyl showed them her little folding pocketknife, it was too much for them and they nearly dissolved. The younger brother had to lean against the truck and daub at his rheumy eyes with a bandanna, and the morning was still so cold that some of the tears were freezing in his eyelashes, which had the effect, in that morning sunlight, of making him look delicate.

Both men wore gloves, and they each took the right one off to shake hands with her and to introduce himself: Bruce, the younger, Ralph, the elder.

"Well, congratulations," Ralph said, grudgingly. "He is a big damn animal."

"Your first, I reckon," said Bruce as he shook her hand — she was surprised by the softness of it, almost a tenderness — Ralph's had been more like a hardened flipper, arthritic and knotted with muscle — and he smiled. "You won't ever shoot one bigger than this," he said.

They rode down to their cabin in the truck, Jyl sitting between them — it seemed odd to her to just go off and leave
the animal lying there in the field — and on the way there,
they inquired tactfully about her life: whether she had a
brother who hunted, or a father, or even a boyfriend. They
asked if her mother was a hunter and it was her turn to
laugh.

"My father used to hunt," she said, and they softened a bit
further.

They made a big breakfast for her — bacon cut from hogs
they had raised and slaughtered, and fried eggs from chickens they likewise kept, and cathead biscuits, and a plate
of delicate pork chops (both men were as lean as match-
sticks, and Jyl marveled at the amount of work the two old
boys must have performed daily, to pour through such fuel
and yet have none of it cling to them) — and after a couple of
cups of black coffee, they gathered up the equipment required for dissembling the elk and drove back up on the hill.

The frost was burning off the grass and the day was warming so that they were able to work without their jackets. Jyl
was struck by how different the brothers seemed, once they
settled into their work: not quite aggressive, but forceful
with their efficiency. And even though they were working
more slowly than usual, in order to explain to her the why
and what of their movements, things still seemed to unfold
quickly.

In a way, it seemed to her that the elk was coming back to
life and expanding, even in its diminishment and unloosen-
ing, the two old men leaning into it like longshoremen, with
Jyl helping them, laboring to roll the beast over on its back,
and inverting the great head with the long daggered antlers,
which now, upended, sank into the freshly furrowed earth

like some mythic harrow fashioned by gods, and one that only certain and select mortals were capable of using, or allowed to use.

And once they had the elk overturned, Ralph emasculated it with his skinning knife, cutting off the ponderous genitals quickly and tossing them farther into the field, with no self-consciousness; it was merely the work that needed doing. And with that same large knife (the handle of which was made of elk antler) he ran the blade up beneath the taut skin from crotch to breastbone while Bruce kept the four legs splayed wide, to give Ralph room to work.

They peeled the hide back to the ribs, as if opening the elk for an operation, or a resuscitation — *How can I ever eat all of this animal?* Jyl wondered — and again, like a surgeon, Bruce placed twin spreader bars between the elk's hocks, bracing wide the front legs as well as the back. Ralph slit open the thick gray-skin drum of fascia that held beneath it the stomach and intestines, heart and lungs and spleen and liver, kidneys and bladder; and then, looking like nothing so much as a grizzly bear grubbing beneath boulders on a hillside, or burrowing, Ralph reached up into the enormous cavity and wrapped both arms around the stomach mass — partially disappearing into the carcass, as if somehow being consumed by it rather than the other way around — and with great effort he was able finally to tug the stomach and all the other internal parts free.

As they pulled loose they made a tearing, ripping, sucking sound, and once it was all out, Ralph and Bruce rolled and cut out with that same sharp knife the oversized heart, as big as a football, and the liver, and laid them out on clean bright butcher paper on the tailgate of their truck.

Then Ralph rolled the rest of the guts, twice as large as

any medicine ball, away from the carcass, pushing it as if shoving some boulder away from a cave's entrance. Jyl was surprised by the sudden focusing of color in her mind, and in the scene. Surely all the colors had been present all along, but for her it was suddenly as if some gears had clicked or aligned, allowing her to notice them now, some subtle rearrangement or recombination blossoming now into her mind's palette: the gold of the wheat stubble and the elk's hide, the dark chocolate of the antlers, the dripping crimson blood midway up both of Ralph's arms, the blue sky, the yellow aspen leaves, the black earth of the field, the purple liver, the maroon heart, Bruce's black and red plaid work shirt, Ralph's faded old denim. The richness of those colors was illuminated so starkly in that October sunlight that it seemed to stir chemicals of deep pleasure in Jyl's own blood, elevating her to a happiness and a fullness she had not known earlier in the day, if quite ever; and she smiled at Bruce and Ralph, and understood in that moment that she, too, was a hunter, might always have been.

She was astounded by how much blood there was: the upended ark of the carcass awash in it, blood sloshing around, several inches deep. Bruce fashioned a come-along around the base of the elk's antlers and hitched the other end to the iron pipe frame on the back of their truck — the frame constructed like a miniature corral, so that they could haul a cow or two to town in the back when they needed to without having to hook up the more cumbersome trailer — and carefully he began to ratchet the elk into a vertical position, an ascension. To Jyl it looked like nothing less than a deification; and again, as a hunter, she found this fitting, and watched with interest.

Blood roared out from the elk's open carcass, gushing out

from between its huge legs, a brilliant fountain in that soft light. The blood splashed and splattered as it hit the new-turned earth — Ralph and Bruce stood by watching the elk drain as if nothing phenomenal at all were happening, as if they had seen it thousands of times before — and the porous black earth drank thirstily this outpouring, this torrent. Bruce looked over at Jyl and said, "Basically, it's easy: you just carve away everything you don't want to eat."

Jyl couldn't take her eyes off how fast the soil was drinking in the blood. Against the dark earth, the stain of it was barely even noticeable.

When the blood had finally stopped draining, Ralph filled a plastic washbasin with warm soapy water from a jug and scrubbed his hands carefully, leisurely, precisely, pausing even to clean the soap from beneath his fingernails with a smaller pocketknife — and when he was done, Bruce poured a gallon jug of clean water over Ralph's hands and wrists to rinse the soap away, and then Ralph dried his hands and arms with a clean towel and emptied out the old bloody wash water, then filled it anew, and it was time for Bruce to do the same. Jyl marveled at, and was troubled by, this privileged glimpse at a life, or two lives, beyond her own — a life, two lives, of cautious competence, fitted to the world; and she was grateful to the elk, and its gone-away life, beyond the sheer bounty of the meat it was providing her, grateful to it for having led her into this place, the small and obscure if not hidden window of these two men's lives.

She was surprised by how mythic the act, and the animal, seemed. She understood intellectually that there were only two acts more ancient — sex and flight — but here was this third one, hunting, suddenly before her. She watched as each man worked with his own knife to peel back the hide, working on each side of the elk simultaneously. Then, with the hide eventually off, they handed it to Jyl and told her it would make a wonderful shirt or robe. She was astonished at the weight of it.

Next they began sawing the forelegs and stout shins of the hind legs; and only now, with those removed, did the creature begin to look reduced or compromised.

Still it rose to an improbable height, the antlers seven feet beyond the eight-foot crossbar of the truck's pole rack — fifteen feet of animal stretched vertically, climbing into the heavens, and the humans working below, so tiny — but as they continued to carve away at it, it slowly came to seem less mythic and more steerlike; and the two old men working steadily upon it began to seem closer to its equal.

They swung the huge shoulders aside, like the wings of an immense flying dinosaur, and then pulled them free, each man wrapping both arms around the slab of shoulder to hold it above the ground. They stacked the shoulders in the truck, next to the rolled-up fur of the hide.

Next the hindquarters, one at a time, severed with a bone saw: both men working together to heft that weight into the truck, and the remaining length of bone and antler and gleaming socket and rib cage looking reptilian, like some reverse evolutionary process, some metamorphic errancy or setback. The pile of beautiful red meat in the back of the truck, though, as it continued to mount, seemed like an embarrassment of riches, and again it seemed to Jyl that perhaps she had taken too much.

She thought how she would have liked to watch her father render an elk. All gone into the past now, however, like blood drawing back into the soil. How much else had she missed?

*

The noonday sun was mild, almost warm now. The scavenger birds — magpies, ravens, Steller's jays and gray jays — danced and hopped nearby, swarming and fluttering, and from time to time as Ralph or Bruce took a rest, one of the men would toss a scrap of gristle or fascia into the field for the birds to fight over, and the sound of their angry squabbles filled the lonely silence of the otherwise quiet and empty hills beneath the thin blue of the Indian summer sky.

They let Jyl work with the skinning knife, showed her how to separate the muscles lengthwise with her fingers before cutting them free of the skeleton, and the quartered ham and shoulder — the backstrap unscrolling beneath the urging of her knife, the meat as dense as stone, it seemed, yet as fluid as a river, and so beautiful in that sunlight, maroon to nearly purple, nearly iridescent in its richness, and in the absence of any intramuscular fat. And now the skeleton, with its whitened bones beginning to show, seemed less an elk, less an animal, than ever; and the two brothers set to work on the neck, and the tenderloins, and butt steaks, and neck loins. And while they separated and then trimmed and butchered those, Jyl worked with her own knife at carving strips of meat from between each slat of rib cage.

From time to time their lower backs would cramp from working so intently and they would have to lie down on the ground, all three of them, looking up at the sky and spreading their arms out wide as if on a crucifix, and would listen to, and feel with pleasure, the subtle popping and realigning of their vertebrae, and would stare up at that blue sky and listen to the cries of the feeding birds, and feel intensely their richness at possessing now so much meat, clean meat, and at simply being alive, with the blood from their labor drying quickly to a light crust on their hands and arms. They were like children, in those moments, and they might easily have napped.

They finished late that afternoon, and sawed the antlers off for Jyl to take home with her. Being old-school, the brothers dragged what was left of the carcass back into the woods, returning it to the forest, returning the skeleton to the very place where the elk had been bedded down when Jyl had first crept up on it — as if she had only borrowed it from the forest for a while — and then they drove back down to their ranch house and hung the ham and shoulder quarters on meat hooks to age in the barn, and draped the backstraps likewise from hooks, where they would leave them for at least a week.

They ran the loose scraps, nearly a hundred pounds' worth, through a hand-cranked grinder, mixed in with a little beef fat to make hamburger, and while Ralph and Jyl processed and wrapped that in two-pound packages, Bruce cooked some of the butt steak in an iron skillet, seasoned with garlic and onions and butter and salt and pepper, mixed with a few of the previous spring's dried morels, reconstituted — and he brought out small plates of that meal, thinly sliced, to eat as they continued working, the three of them grinding and wrapping, and the mountain of meat growing on the table beside them. They each had a tumbler of whiskey to sip as they worked, and when they finally finished it was nearly midnight.

The brothers offered their couch to Jyl and she accepted; they let her shower first, and they built a fire for her in the wood stove next to the couch. After Bruce and then Ralph had showered, they sat up visiting, each with another small glass of whiskey, Ralph and Bruce telling her their ancient histories until none of them could stay awake — their eyes kept closing, and their heads kept drooping — and with the fire burning down, Ralph and Bruce roused from their chairs and made their way each to his bedroom, and Jyl pulled the old elk hides over her for warmth and fell deeply and immediately asleep, falling as if through some layering of time, and with her hunting season already over, that year. That elk would not be coming back, and her father would not be coming back. She was the only one remaining with those things safe and secure in her now. For a while.

She killed more elk, and deer, too, in seasons after that, learning more about them, year by year, in the killing, than she could ever learn otherwise. Ralph died of a heart attack several years later and was buried in the yard outside the ranch house, and Bruce died of pneumonia the next year, overwhelmed by the rigors of twice the amount of work, and he, too, was buried in the yard, next to Ralph, in an aspen grove, through which passed on some nights wandering herds of deer and elk, the elk direct descendants of the big bull Jyl had shot, and which the brothers had dismembered and then shared with her, the three of them eating on it for well over a year. The elk sometimes pausing to gnaw at the back of those aspen with roots that reached now for the chests of the buried old men.

Remembering these things, a grown woman now woven of losses and gains, Jyl sometimes looks down at her body and considers the mix of things: the elk becoming her, as she ate it, and becoming Ralph and Bruce, as they ate it (did this make them somehow, distantly, like brothers and sister, or uncles and niece, if not fathers and daughter?) — and the two old men becoming the soil then, in their burial, as had her father, becoming as still and silent as stone, except for the worms that writhed now in their chests, and her own tenuous memories of them. And her own gone-away father, worm food, elk food, now: but how he had loved it.

Mountains in her heart now, and antlers, and mountain lions and sunrises and huge forests of pine and spruce and tamarack, and elk, all uncontrollable. She likes to think now that each day she moves farther away from him, she is also moving closer to him.

As if within her, beneath the span of her own days, there are other hunts going on continuously, giant elk in flight from the pursuit of hunters other than herself, and the birth of other mountains being plotted and planned — other mountains rising, then, and still more mountains vanishing into distant seas — and that even more improbable than her encountering that one giant elk, on her first hunt, was the path, the wandering line, that brought her to her father in the first place, that delivered her to him and had made him hers and she his — the improbability and yet the certainty that would place the two of them in each other's lives, tiny against the backdrop of the world and tinier still against the mountains of time.

But belonging to each other, as much in death as in life. Inescapably, and forever. The hunt showing her that.

YAZOO

THE FIRST TIME I realized that Wejumpka was strong, really strong, was when I slept in late. It was a rainy morning in November, late in the morning — almost noon. Vern and I had been up drinking, talking, playing records, until well past three-thirty in the morning. The doctors had said that Vern could go any month now, any week, even; that when his liver shut down everything bad was going to start happening, real fast. That was just the way it was, though, and you couldn't change a man's whole life.

"It's like trying to make a pine tree turn into an oak," Vern said about his not being able to stop drinking. We weren't drinking anything hard: just beer, to remind us of when we were young, and because there'd been a sale on it that day at the gas station.

Vern's most recent girlfriend, a girl my age, a girl I'd gone to high school with, had left him two days ago, saying she didn't want to be around when he died; but Vern finally understood that he was indeed going to die, that it was coming, no maybes about it, and he had decided that there was a sort of dignity in not changing his movements, his patterns, before it happened. He didn't want to feel like he was running from it, since it was going to happen, and though I had not agreed with his logic at first, I saw what he was talking about the closer we got to it. Or I thought I did. He said that he did not miss the girl much one way or the other, if that was how she was, and I saw what he meant by that, too.

It was almost as if it was all happening to me instead of to him; I could see all of it, could see why he was doing things. It was what anyone would have done.

We kept the beers iced down in a trash can, floated them in water and ice, and they were so cold that they made our teeth hurt. Sometimes Vern would cry out in pain when he got up to go to the restroom. It was a bad thing he had done to himself, all that drinking, but it was done and there wasn't any going back.

"It's like a ski run," I said, "coming down a long run, near the bottom, where you haven't fallen yet. You can try jumps, loops, flips, anything. You're hot, you're on a roll, you can do anything."

"I've never been skiing before," Vern said. He looked down at his beer. He was fifty, but looked sixty-five. His face was loose on him, and his eyes were sad and red, and his hair had gone all to hell, shot through with gray where it wasn't falling out; but he still had Wejumpka, his youngest, and always would. Instead of talking about dying, we talked about Wejumpka whenever the subject of Vern's health came up. I was Wejumpka's godfather, next in line, and it scared me.

"How're you doing, big guy?" I'd ask, putting a hand on Vern's shoulder. I'm thirty, but feel older.

And Vern would grin, glad I was gripping his shoulder, and he'd look down and say something like, "That Wejumpka, he's something else."

Wejumpka was twelve. Vern had another son, Austin, who was eighteen by then, but Austin was different. Austin had run away from home when he was sixteen to Arizona to live on an Indian reservation and take peyote; Austin drank like a fish, had a marijuana plant growing in the backyard of his mother's house, sassed his mother, wore earrings, and was, we suspected, asexual.

But Wejumpka! My godson built model planes, wrote his thank-you notes, hugged everyone he met, and sometimes sat on the back porch with his dog, a big golden retriever named Ossie, and played the harmonica. He was learning to play it well.

It's a quiet neighborhood, full of old trees, Spanish moss, everything moving slow. The houses were two and three stories, with their foundations thrown down in what was then forest, built on the treacherous, shifting Yazoo clay formation: slick and red, deceitful, it was beginning to crawl back toward the swamp, toward the Pearl River, trying to take the houses with it.

A lot of the homes were for sale. There were small panics at the first crack in the driveway, the crack that grew after a rainstorm or a cold spell, sometimes growing so fast that you thought you could see it happening.

Vern wasn't supposed to be anywhere near Ann. The judge had barred him from coming within a five-mile radius of her; he'd given Vern a map of the city of Jackson, showing where he could and could not go. It was simply too much for the city to bear, otherwise. Vern and Ann went at it like cats and dogs, hissing and spitting whenever they came across each other, throwing canned goods at each other, turning one another's shopping carts over in the grocery store. Vern had sometimes shopped with the red-haired girl who was now gone, which had infuriated Ann to new levels of ber-serkness — she was a big woman, getting bigger since the divorce, and she'd take her Mace sprayer out of her purse and chase Vern through the grocery store with it, spraying him as if he were a bad dog — and it was just too much for the city to stand.

But I wasn't barred from being in the neighborhood, and because so many of the shifting homes were up for sale, some of them were also available for lease and for rent: for anything. Most people just wanted out, any way they could do it. Quitting was imminent.

To help Vern out and to keep an eye on his boy, and on old Ann, I rented the house across the street; put curtains up, wore a false beard and mustache and wig, walked with a limp and a cane, so she would not know it was me.

I can't really stress enough how brutal the divorce was. It took everything they both had, and then from Vern it took a little more.

Ann got his new unlisted phone number and passed it out to her friends. They would call him at all hours of the night — and always he had to answer, not knowing if it was an emergency involving one of the boys or merely another hate call — but always it was the latter.

"You're a dead man, Davidson," a woman's husky voice

would whisper, full of hate: maniacal, and full of the holiness of being right. "Dead *meat*," the voice would hiss, and then hang up. And Vern would laugh about it, telling it to me, but he had also half worried about it for a long time — and months later, when the calls finally stopped coming, he had begun to worry even more, as if now they didn't dare risk threatening him, because they were *serious* now and didn't want him to be alert.

He listened to noises in the night for a long time, he said, and wondered how they would do it to him. He couldn't understand such hatred; he would shake his head, run his hand through his hair, and say, "I just don't get it. It was only a divorce."

I wanted to tell him that it was *not* just a divorce, that it was all these lives, that they were ticking away, lost time, misspent hours, and things ruined, good things — but that was precisely what Ann's angry friends were telling him, and I was Vern's pal so I could not do that. I had to try to bolster him, even if with stories, tales and lies, until he was back on his feet again, or until the end. It was a hard job.

If Vern was out, Ann's friends would leave messages on his answering machine. They called from pay phones, and when they got the answering machine, they would tell him to check with Sue at the hospital, that there'd been an accident involving one of the boys.

He had been wrong, but they were more wrong. They were guerrilla tactics, brutal and nasty, and I did not blame Vern for wanting to get out early. I opened his beers for him, handed them to him, got the whiskey for him out of the freezer. I'd always heard that a weak man can stand any kind of pain except another's. I didn't know if I was being weak. It was the only thing I knew to do. Reason had long ago left

Ann and would never return; and Vern's strength, and courage, had finally been worn down.

There was only my godchild, Wejumpka, left.

We drove into the garage after dark, wearing dark clothes, sometimes already drunk, and pulled the garage door down and made sure all the curtains were drawn before turning on any lights inside. We always kept one man at the window upstairs in a room with the lights turned off, to keep an eye on his house. It was usually Vern up there.

I'd be down in the kitchen fixing supper, or fixing drinks, and he'd be sitting backwards on a chair, resting over it like a riverboat captain, watching his old house with expensive field glasses, the kind hunters use right at dusk for drawing in as much of the failing light as possible — and he'd call out in a loud voice what all was going on, a radio announcer giving the play-by-play.

If Ann was in the kitchen he could see her, and he'd call out what she was cooking, what she was nibbling on — "She's feeding her fat face with *croutons*," he'd howl; "She's just eating the croutons out of the box with her paw, like a *primate!*" he'd roar, sometimes falling backwards, and I'd have to rush up to see if he was all right, to clean up the beer he'd spilled and to hand him another — but other times he would fall silent, and downstairs, hearing the silence, I'd know that he must have the binoculars trained on the boys, if Austin was home: that perhaps they were lying on the rug in the den in front of the television, or maybe simply even doing their homework.

One time I brought drinks upstairs, Long Island iced teas in tall glasses, with another gallon of reserves in a pitcher, and some nachos, only to find him weeping, still watching the house across the street through the field glasses, but with tears rolling down his cheeks and shoulders shaking.

The curtains were open across the street, and in the yellow square of light in Ann's living room we could see Austin trying to teach Wejumpka how to dance to some song we could not hear.

We could only watch, as if they were an old silent film, while Austin, with his raggedy blue-jean jacket and old Levis, his long woman's hair and earrings, shut his eyes and boogied madly, running in place, it seemed, throwing his arms up in the air and shaking them in a free, mad glee, and then stopping, suddenly, standing behind Wejumpka, lifting Wejumpka's arms, trying to show Wejumpka how it was done, growing exasperated, then, when Wejumpka did not get the hang of it. Austin stepped in front of Wejumpka once more and began dancing again, writhing and jumping, leaping, doubtless to one of Vern's old records that Ann had confiscated. All the old good ones were in there. It was probably Bob Seger, I thought, but said nothing, and pulled the shades so Vern wouldn't have to watch any longer.

We noticed that Ann was having to turn sideways to get through doorways. She was Vern's and my height, five foot eight or so, and had been a pretty plump 160 pounds at the wedding, and 185 soon thereafter; during the months preceding the divorce, Vern said, she had weighed in at around 240, and now, almost three years later, she had to be tipping them at close to 300 and was showing no signs of slowing down.

"Would you have loved her if she were not fat?" I asked Vern. He leaned back and roared with laughter, shaking with it, delighted with the thought, and with the simplicity of such an idea.

One day we watched as the carpenters came and widened all her doorways for her, so that she could fit through them more easily. I wondered if it embarrassed Wejumpka to have a mother so large; I wondered what he thought about Vern's breath, about Vern always being drunk.

But Wejumpka still seemed to be his usual self. It was almost as if he thought that these things did not matter, or that they were of a lesser importance — though I had no idea what, then, he thought *was* important. Sometimes we'd watch the house on weekends, in the broad middle of the day, though it was riskier; and we'd open the windows in the fall just to get some fresh air moving through the rented house and to listen to the street and neighborhood sounds — lawn mowers, boys raking, motor scooters, the whole fall list — and in the late afternoon we could hear Wejumpka sitting on the back porch playing his harmonica; a faint sound of which we heard only parts, while the rest of it was washed down the street along with tumbling dry leaves by the winds that moved through the neighborhood.

"He's blowing it like a signal," Vern would say. There is no excusing a drunk, no reasoning with him, and he'd be certain of it, swearing up and down and crying that Wejumpka wanted to see him, that that was the reason he was out there by himself playing the harmonica, and Vern would jump up and go tearing down the stairs, pulling his jacket on, running as if to rescue Wejumpka from a burning house, running out into the purple gloom of dusk and across the street, out into the crisp night, and I'd be running behind him, trying to catch up and to keep him from harm.

Vern's shirttail would be out, his shoelaces untied, his jacket on inside out; he'd go tearing through the hedge toward Wejumpka, who, thank God, was always alone, always playing the harmonica by himself and sometimes even humming or singing. Had Ann seen Vern that close to the center of the demilitarized zone, that far into it, she would surely have taken the hoe to him, with no emotion whatsoever, merely striking at him as she would a weed until he was no longer there — but she never saw him, and Vern would crawl under the bushes, through the hedge, and creep toward Wejumpka, crawling to stay out of Ann's sight, and he'd go all the way up to where Wejumpka was sitting and rest his head on Wejumpka's knee, reach up and tousle his hair, squeeze his shoulder, and say, "Hi, pal. How's it going?"

I do not think that Wejumpka ever associated his harmonica playing with these appearances by Vern. I do not think he ever realized that he was *summoning* Vern, like a bad genie from a bottle, by blowing the wistful notes; I think he merely played the harmonica and hummed as a way of breathing, of *feeling;* in the evenings, when it began to grow dark and things were not quite so clear, he would go sit with his dog, and hum, and sing. He had a fine, clear voice, though his harmonica playing was still a little unsure, a little quavery.

He was always glad to see his father, though I could tell by the way he looked back at the house that his mother had instructed him, in her fat intuitiveness, what he should do if his father ever *did* approach him. But then he would look back down at Vern and put his harmonica down, smiling, and would pat Vern's mussed-up hair, smoothing it into place, patting Vern as if he were a dog, while he patted Ossie with his other hand.

They'd sit there like that, with night coming down and stars coming up through the trees, until I could stand the tension no longer; and I'd come out of the bushes and help

Vern sit up, and tell Wejumpka that we had to go now, and, strangely, Vern always let me take him, never put up a struggle. It was not that he feared Ann, I think, but more that he was simply relaxed at having seen his son again, at just having *touched* him and talked to him for a while, petted the dog together with him and asked him how school was going, if the other kids were treating him okay, so that Vern would then do anything I told him to: he'd be tired from the drinking, but, more important, just out and out utterly relaxed, utterly happy, and I could lead him away, back the way we had come, crawling into the dark hedge and then sneaking back across the street to our rented spy house.

"You'll remember not to bother your mother with this, right?" I'd ask my godson, and he'd nod, looking down at his feet, too soon an adult, and say, "Sure, sure." At first he'd wanted to call me Uncle Mac, but Vern and I had gotten him to drop the Uncle, and it made him seem like even more of an adult, sometimes.

Vern was still working, right on through his illness; there would be the insurance money afterward, but until then there was always the alimony, and some months it was such a tight squeeze, he could barely make it.

We'd watch Ann in the evenings, sometimes eating a whole brick of cheese in front of the kitchen window, staring over the sink, gnawing at it, eating the whole slab, looking back over her shoulder to see if either of the children was coming. Or angel food cake — she'd buy them at the grocery store instead of making them, and simply bury her whole face in one, eating her way through the middle until her face appeared on the other side, looking like some sort of clown's, and Vern would begin howling again, slapping his leg and laughing, falling out of the chair again, but I did not think it was so funny, sometimes; even from across the street, I could feel Ann's panic, and it made me hungry, made me want to eat something, too — but instead I would get up and fix more drinks.

I slept so late that morning in November not because of the previous night's drinking but because it was raining and I liked the sound of it. I liked having the big rented house and the chance to help someone out, even if I was on the wrong side. It made me feel like an outlaw, a desperado, which I had never been before, and I liked it. The rain on someone else's house, with me warm and dry inside, made me feel like a bank robber holed up in a cave somewhere.

I was against the law, though not as much as some, and I liked it; and I was only a renter, borrowing someone else's house. If things turned sour, I could flee; I could leave like a leaf tumbling down the street, tumbling into the woods, away from the sliding houses.

So I slept, smiling, warm and dry, with my hands behind my head, and I was a little frightened of what would happen when Vern passed on, when his liver finally stopped straining and I was responsible for his son — that thought would come at me from all directions, frightening me — but then I'd remember that Vern's liver had *not* stopped straining and filtering, not yet, that he was asleep downstairs, and he would be until three or four in the afternoon, and I could go back to sleep, listening to the rain, which was coming down in a steady, soothing wash.

I knew that the other people in the neighborhood, the ones with homes, children, and futures, had to be distressed — because when the Yazoo clay got wet, when it got loaded with water, it would start to move again, sliding down the hill, pulling the houses and driveways and foundations with it, slowly — an inch a month during the rainy seasons of winter and spring, like some inept magician's tablecloth trick — but that was none of my worry, none at all, and it was only those people's bad luck, or just plain bad planning, that had made them build there, and none of it had anything to do with me.

Still, it made me feel guilty. After about eleven o'clock in the morning I couldn't sleep anymore, and I got up and moved over to the window to see how hard it was raining, and I was surprised to see that it was raining much harder than I'd expected: a steady, straight, hard-falling rain, with no wind, a rain that was backing up the gutters and flooding the streets, and starting to lap up into the yards.

Small children in diapers were sitting out in the middle of the street, waist deep, laughing and splashing and playing with yellow rubber ducks, as if the street were their bathtub. It made me hate Mississippi, then; I thought of how the sewage system would be stopping up, losing pressure, and would be backing its materials up into these same waters. The parents were out there with their children, wearing raincoats and rubber boots, holding umbrellas, laughing, silly, oblivious — thinking, perhaps, that this time their houses were not going to slide, and that all water was clean, all water was good, thinking that they were *lucky* because their street had decided to turn into a river, a river that flowed right past their houses, not understanding how dangerous any of it was. The children could be getting typhoid, salmonella, or worse. The young parents were just standing out there in the rain, ankle deep in the water, laughing.

They should have all been feeling like outlaws — it was making my breathing fast and shallow, just to think about it.

Just because these people could afford to buy big houses and clothes for their children, to send them to private schools and such, did not mean they were safe. They were like hens, all of them, just gathered out in the barnyard, pecking grain, with Thanksgiving coming on. I was so mad that Vern was dying. When he was gone there would be no one; just his sons, but it would be a long time before they became him, before they filled his place, pouring into his space like water flowing into a footprint left in the mud, flowing across it, then covering it . . .

But Wejumpka's strength! He was wearing his Indian headdress and whittling on a stick of balsa wood. He looked like an adult, even with the headdress on, sitting back up on the porch out of the rain, watching the other children play. I picked up the field glasses and focused them on the kitchen behind him, and saw Ann eating chocolate ice cream out of the carton with a spoon, watching the children, too, and watching their parents. Ann ate slowly, transfixed, I think, by the sight of young couples, of married couples, of a man and a woman, together; though it's possible, too, that she was seeing nothing, only tasting the ice cream — or maybe standing very still, very firm, and trying to feel if the clay was beginning to slide under her house.

A station wagon came driving up, creeping slowly through the street's floodwaters, sending rocking muddy waves out from either side of it, washing water up into people's yards, moving down the street like a boat, and I recognized it as Wejumpka's carpool, though it was not a school day.

It stopped in front of Wejumpka's house, parking in a puddle, and children began piling out of it, more children than I ever imagined, all wearing rubber boots and raincoats, and they ran up to Wejumpka's porch, jumping and laughing, delighted to see him, and I was amazed.

Just a year ago he had been unpopular, had been teased unmercifully — teased about his name, teased about the way he hugged everyone, teased about his father, the drunkest man in town — but this was different, this was unexpected, and they had him up on their shoulders, then, and were carrying him, headdress and all, out into the rain, and the woman who'd driven the carpool was out with them, helping set up these sawhorses, across which she and another child placed a wide plank board that had been sticking out of the back of the station wagon.

A little girl was there to take pictures; the carpool driver held an umbrella over her as she adjusted her camera, very seriously, very professionally, taking light readings and motioning the other children into their places.

Wejumpka, looking not so much thrilled or even happy, but more bored than anything, shrugged his shoulders and moved where she wanted him, into his position beneath the plank, sort of squatting, bent over, with his back pressed up against the plank, then, and all the other children whooping and shouting, pulling one another's hair and kicking, climbing up onto the plank — all of them, and I counted seven, eight, nine — and I figured that if they weighed seventy pounds each, average, that was more than six hundred pounds, and it would truly be an amazing feat, if he could do it, and I wanted to call the newspaper, the television stations, and everyone I knew.

I was flabbergasted.

Ann had turned away from the window before the station wagon had pulled up, had gone back into the den and was watching television, having taken the ice cream carton with her, and was still spooning the stuff into her mouth; she seemed to take no notice. I opened the window so that I could hear what was going on down in the yard. The cold rain beat against my face; it was starting to blow past in sheets. The other children in the street, the rubber duck children and their parents, had glanced over but then turned away, as if not realizing what was going on, either.

The little school photographer had her flash attachment rigged up, and had it all ready, crouching down, and was telling Wejumpka to "Do it," to "Do it!" I wondered why they had picked this of all days to shoot the picture; there must have been some sort of deadline. I wanted to call down to Vern to try to rouse him, but I did not want to miss a thing.

The rain was whipping in then, harder than ever, sometimes obscuring the street, and the children out in Ann's yard. The rubber duckers were screaming, gathering their toys and children and running for their houses, stung by the hard pellets as the rain turned to hail. I could see the flashbulb popping; the pictures were being taken, but I couldn't see if Wejumpka was making the lift or not.

I thought I could hear cheering and whistling, clapping, but I wasn't sure. It could have been the wind.

And then the wind had blown the curtains of hail past and I could see again, and Wejumpka *did* have the plank off the sawhorses: it was up on his back, his stout little legs braced wide apart and quivering, trembling, and his eyes squeezed shut, his face trembling and turning red, but he had them all up in the air, they were all resting on his back, and the little photographer was moving in closer, getting different angles, vertical and horizontal shots for the school paper, getting below him and shooting directly up into the hail. But no one else was out, just the one teacher and all the children: only the children seemed to know what Wejumpka was doing, what was going on.

Vern was asleep, drunk to the world, sleeping through the last part of his life, drooling; and I looked beyond Wejumpka's heroic tremblings, looked down into the den, and could see that Ann had taken her blouse off and was lying by the fire, smearing the ice cream all over herself, and that she, too, had her eyes closed. I stared, horrified, trying to read the lips as she murmured something, and I picked up the field glasses and trained them on her.

The ice cream was melting and running all over her.

I could read her lips. "Me, me," she was murmuring. "Me, me, me."

I saw how she would never let up, not until Vern was dead, and that even then she would hate him for his betrayal, and would be bitter; and that she did not care what her hatred of him was doing to her son, that it was just too strong for her alone to handle.

Wejumpka continued to stand out in the hailstorm, trembling, shuddering, trying to impress his new friends, while slowly his house, and the one across the street, slid swampward, riding on the slick Yazoo clay.

THE CANOEISTS

THE TWO OF THEM would go canoeing on any of the many winding creeks and rivers that braided their way through the woods and gentle hills to the north. They would drive north in Bone's old truck and put the boat on the Brazos, or the Colorado, or White Oak Creek, or even the faster-running green waters of the Guadalupe, without a care of where they might end up, and would explore those unknown seams of water and bright August light with no maps, knowing only what lay right before them as they rounded each bend.

They would take wine, and a picnic lunch, and fishing tackle, and a lantern. They drifted beneath high chalky bluffs, beneath old bridges, and past country yards where children playing tag on the hillsides among trees above the river stopped to watch them pass. They paddled on, Bone shirtless in the stern and Sissy straw-hatted in the bow, in her swimsuit. When they reached sun-scrubbed bars of white sand next to deep, dark pools, around the bend from any town or road, shaded by towering oaks, they would beach the canoe and lie on blankets in the sun like basking turtles, sweating nude, glistening, drinking wine and getting up every now and again to run down to the river and dive in, to cleanse the suntan oil and grit of sand and shine of sex from their bodies.

Hot breezes would dry their bodies quickly again, once they returned to the blankets. Their damp hair would keep them cool for a little while. They would lie perfectly still on their backs, looking up at the sun, hands clasped, and listen to the shouts, the sawing buzz, of the seventeen-year locusts going insane back in the forest, choking on the heat.

Later, when the day had cooled slightly — when the tops of the trees were beginning to catch and block some of the sun's direct rays — they would climb back into the green canoe and drift farther downstream, unconcerned by the notions or constraints of time and the amount of water that had passed by. If anything, they felt nourished and enriched by it.

They would paddle on into dusk, and then into the night, falling deeper in love, and speaking even less, as night fell; paddling with the lantern lit and balanced on the bow, with moths following them — they had no idea where they were — while Bone would cast to fish, sometimes catching one slash-silver fighting and leaping just outside the glow cast by the lantern's ring of light.

Fireflies would line the banks, illuminating the route they should take — the fireflies would not venture over water, so the darkness of their absence was a winding lane for them —

and they passed too occasionally the bright window-square blazons of farmhouses, of families tucked in for the night, also lining both edges of the shore.

When they came to a lonely bridge or railroad trestle, they would finally relinquish the day, or that part of it, to the river, and eddy out to the bank, where Sissy would climb out with the lantern and Bone would pass her the equipment, and then he would climb out and shoulder the canoe like some shell-bound brute, and they would pick their way up the slope, clambering through brush and litter tossed from decades of the bridge's passersby, ascending to the road and firm level ground while the river below kept running past.

Owls would be hooting, and heat lightning, like a pulse or an echo from the day's troubles — or like a price that must be paid for the day's bliss — would be shuddering in distant sky-flash in all directions, though it seemed like no price or debt or accounting to Bone and Sissy, only more blessing, as the breezes from the far-off thunderstorms stirred and cooled them as they walked through cricket-song and darkness, save for those glimmers of lightning and the fireflies that dotted the meadows and swarmed around the couple as if accompanying them. They might be five miles from their truck, or they might be twenty; how to get there, they would have no idea, but neither would they be worried: Bone would not be due back at work for another twelve hours.

They would walk down the center of the dark road, Bone toting the canoe over his head like a crucifix, or some huge umbrella, and Sissy walking beside him, feeling love for him as a human but also with the comfortable affection and unspoken communication one has with animals: a dog, a horse, a gentle bull, a cat. And she felt much the same herself —

part human, but part other-animal, as well — and it was, again, the calmest she could ever remember being.

After a while a vehicle would approach from one direction or another, almost always an old truck in that section of the country, and the driver would give them a ride. They would lash the canoe in belly-side down, as if it were still in the water, and climb up into the cab with the old farmer and ride back north into the night, though other times when there was no rope they would sit in the canoe itself, in the back, slanted skyward, gripping both the canoe's gunwales and the side of the truck to keep it from sliding out. They would ride seated in the canoe, wind rushing past them at forty, fifty miles an hour, and would be unafraid, too deep in love to know anything beyond the beauty of the moment, their hair swirling and the rolls of lightning-wash flashing.

Sometimes their patron, as he crossed a county line, would want to stop at the neon red of a bar — only a handful of other old trucks parked out in front — and they would climb out of the canoe to go inside with him, to share a beer, and perhaps a sandwich, or ribs. The sides of their green canoe would be smeared with the wind-crushed bodies from the swarms of fireflies they'd driven through, some of them still glowing gold but becoming dimmer, as if cooling, and it made the canoe look special, and pretty, like a float in some parade, and people in the bar would come to the doorway and stare for a moment at it thus decorated, and at Bone and Sissy — as if someone special, or important, or simply charmed had come to visit.

They would drink a beer, would shoot a game or two of pool, and would visit in the dark bar, listening to the jukebox while the summer storm moved in and thundered across and past, like the nighttime passage of some huge herd of animals above. And afterward, when they went back out and climbed into their canoe to head on back north, with the driver searching for where they had left their truck, the air would be scrubbed clean and cooler, and steam would be rising from the dark roads, and the smears of fireflies would be washed from their canoe so that all was dark around them again.

They would find their truck, eventually, and would thank the old driver, and shake his hand, and for the rest of his short days he would remember having given them a ride, as they would likewise remember it for the rest of their long days; and what invisible braid or fabric is formed of such connections, transitory and sprawling across time, across generations? Do they last, invisible, to form a kind of fiber or residue in the world, or are they all eventually washed away, as if cleansed and made nothing again by a summer rainstorm's passage?

They would drive home toward the big city with the windows rolled down, listening to the radio. They would unload the canoe when they got to Bone's house and climb the stairs without bothering to turn on any of the lights. It might be two or three A.M. They would undress and climb into his bed, into the familiar clean sheets — warmer, upstairs — and open the windows for fresh air, and would make love again, both for the pleasure of it as well as to somehow seal or anchor their return home; and at daylight Bone would awaken and shower and dress in his suit, and head to work, leaving Sissy still asleep in his bed, their bed, swirled in white cotton sheets and asleep in a wash of morning sunshine.

THE LIVES OF ROCKS

Things improved, as the doctors had promised they would. She still got winded easily, and her strength wasn't returning (her digestion would never be the same, they warned her; her intestines had been scalded, cauterized as if by volcanic flow), but she was alive, and between spells of fear and crying she was able to take short walks, stopping to rest often, making her walks not on the craggy mountain where she had once hiked, but on the gentle slope behind her house that led through mature forest to a promontory above a rushing creek.

There was a picnic table up there, and a fire ring, and sometimes she would take her blanket and a book up there, and build a fire for warmth, and nestle into a slight depression in the ground, and read, and sleep. On the way up to the picnic table she would have to stop several times to catch her breath — when she stopped and lay down in the pine needles she felt that the world was still carrying her along, al-

though once she reached that promontory and built her little fire and settled in to her one spot, she felt fixed in the
world again, as if she were a boulder in midstream, around
which the current parted: and it was a spot she strove to
reach, every day, though some days it took her several hours
just to travel that short distance, and there were other days
when she could not get there at all.

She slept at least as much as she had when she was a baby.
Some days it was all she could do to get to the hospital for
her daily treatment, so that the days were broken into but
two segments, the twenty hours of sleep and the four hours
of treatment, including the commute to the hospital.

Her nearest neighbors were a fundamentalist Christian
family named Workman, a name that had always made her
laugh, for she had rarely seen them *not* working: the mother,
the father, and the five children — three boys and two girls,
ranging in age from fourteen to two.

The Workmans lived only a few miles away as a raven flew,
though it was many miles by rutted road to drive to the head
of their valley — and even then a long walk in was required.
They lived without electricity or running water or indoor
plumbing or refrigeration or telephone, and they often were
without a car that ran. They owned five acres downstream
along the creek, the same creek that Jyl lived by, in the next
valley over, and they had a fluctuating menagerie of chickens, milk cows, pigs, goats, horses, ponies, and turkeys.

When they traveled to town, which was not often, difficult
as it was for them to get out of their valley, they were as likely
to ride single file on a procession of odd-sized and strangely
colored, strangely shaped horses and ponies as they were to
travel in one of their decrepit vehicles, smoke rings issuing

from both the front and back ends as it chugged down the ragged road.

No family ever worked harder, and it seemed to Jyl sometimes that their God was a god of labor rather than mercy or forgiveness. When she saw them on the road, they were usually working — often pulled over in the shade of cottonwoods, dipping water from a puddle to pour into their steaming radiator, or stopped with their small remuda haltered to a grove of trees while they examined some injury to one of the horses' or ponies' hoofs — and even when all was well and the horses, or truck, were in motion, Jyl had noticed that they were ceaselessly working: the girls riding in the back of the truck, knitting or sewing small deer hide knickknacks to try to sell at the People's Market, the boys husking corn or shelling peas or cracking nuts, their fingers always moving, always working, in a way that reminded Jyl of the way that she herself had addressed the mountain before, with her long strides just as relentless.

From the Workmans' cabin came the sounds of industry at all hours of the day: the buzz of chain saws, the crashing of timber, the splitting of wood, the jingle-trace rattling of mules in chains pulling stumps and stoneboats to carve out ever more garden space in the side of the rocky hillside, the mountain beneath which they lived. They were forever adding on this or that strange-shaped loft or closet or cubicle to accommodate their ever-expanding brood, as well as the developing needs for space and privacy among their older children, so that the steady sounds of those renovations filled their little valley, and the smoke from burning stumps and piles of slash and smoldering stubble fields, as well as from their various wood stove chimneys, rose from that cove day and night, in all seasons, as if just over the mountain there were some long and inconclusive war being waged, or as if such a battle had just finished and only the ruins remained now, still smoking — though always, the next day, the sounds resumed: the clangings and bangings, the shouts and orders and complaints, the buzzing and grinding, the hammering and sawing, backfires and outbursts . . .

On her hikes to the top of the mountain and back, particularly late in the autumn when the leaves had fallen from the deciduous trees, opening up greater views of the countryside, there had been a space where Jyl had been able to look down from one of the deer-trail paths that ran along the high cliffs and see into the Workmans' little valley, and it had seemed to her that the dominant activity on that little landscape, and in that isolated little family, had been the gathering of firewood — always, there were children trundling from out of the woods, their arms filled with ricks of limbs and branches — and, if not that, the gathering of water: the children traveling back and forth to the river, ferrying double-bucketful loads with each trip, trudging slowly and carefully to avoid sloshing too much but spilling some nonetheless — the younger children having to set the buckets down frequently to stop and rest, and to massage their stretched-out arms.

And in berry-picking season, the entire slope of the mountainside seemed covered with Workmans, wearing straw hats against the bright sun and faded sun-soft overalls, dropping their berries one by one into straw baskets, and down at their home there would be smoke rising from the chimneys on even the hottest summer days, as the mother, Sarah, boiled water for sterilizing the canning jars and for boiling the berries down to make preserves and jam. Jyl would watch them as she hiked up the mountain, observing them in little glimpses through the trees, in all seasons, and she would pass on by.

She remembered a game she had played as a child, often while waiting for her father to come back from the wilderness: from the Far North, from the Andes, from China and Mongolia — from all the wildernesses of the world, all the treasured storehouses of elemental wealth.

She had constructed paper boats and then sent them downstream in the little mountain creeks, running along beside them, following them for as long as she could, hurdling logs and boulders, pretending that the toy boats were ships bound for sea, ships on which she should have been a passenger — voyages for which she had a ticket, but with the ship having embarked without her. And though she knew it was only the skewed and selective memory of childhood, it seemed to her that that was how she had spent most of her time then, chasing after those bobbing, pitching little boats of her own making.

Seeking partly to provide entertainment and even a touch of magic for the hardened lives of the Workman children living downstream from her — and seeking also some contact with the outside world — she began to craft little boats once again, while waiting at the hospital, or at home, at night, in the last few minutes before sleep, seeking to integrate something new into her life other than sleep and pain.

As if these little boats would bring her father back, where nothing else had before.

She whittled the boats out of willow and pine — catamarans, canoes, battleships, destroyers, yachts, and pleasure boats — and scrolled up little notes inside dollhouse milk bottles, dated and signed, "Your neighbor on the other side of the mountain," and sealed them with candle wax before launching them; and as she had so long ago, she hurried alongside them through the snow and ice, as best as she could: though she had to stop quickly now, due to the breathlessness.

On the notes inside the bottles, she had penned increasingly impressionistic entries, commenting on the beauty of the season, the wonder of the landscape, and the goodness of life in general. She crafted increasingly intricate vessels, and took pleasure in doing so — though as the weeks passed and the children did not come to visit her, she had pretty much given up hope that her vessels and their messages would ever be found, and she figured that even if they were, it would be by someone so much farther downstream that the identification "Your neighbor over the mountain" would have no meaning.

And that was all right, she supposed. It was enough for her to be speaking out to the rest of the world, to the wider world — enough to be striving for some other contact, to be reaching out from within the darkness that threatened to envelop her, and to be testifying, even if to a perhaps unseeing future, about the beauties she was still witnessing, even in her fear. Perhaps someone — perhaps the Workman children themselves — would find the ships far into the future, as adults. It didn't matter. It was enough for Jyl to be making beautiful little carvings — no matter that only the rivers and forests themselves might be all who ever saw them, like prayers not so much to a god who did not exist, but to one who simply chose not to respond.

So she was surprised when the fifteen-year-old boy and his seven-year-old sister knocked at her door one afternoon, waking her from a deep sleep.

There were still a couple of hours of daylight left, and it was snowing lightly. Snow was mantled on the backs and shoulders of the children. "Come in," she said. "I would have thought you'd be out hunting, in this good snow."

The boy, Stephan, looked surprised. "We've already got our animals," he said, though the season had only been open a couple of weeks. He paused. "Have you?"

Jyl shook her head. "I haven't been out yet."

A look of concern crossed the boy's face and, to a lesser degree, the girl's. "You're going, aren't you?"

Jyl smiled. "Maybe," she said.

Stephan just stared at her, as if unable to conceive of a life in which meat, free meat, could be turned down, or not even pursued.

The girl, Shayna, took off her pack. Jyl had assumed both of their packs were loaded with extra coats and scarves and mittens — a flashlight, perhaps, and a loaf of bread — but instead there were her ships, every one of them.

"We were thinking if we brought them back you can maybe send them to us again," Shayna said.

Stephan rattled the little glass bottles in his pocket, fished them out and held them before her, a double handful. "We liked the notes," he said. "We're pasting them into a scrapbook. They look real nice. I'm not sure we got the ships and messages in the right order, but they kind of tell a story anyway." He handed her back the bottles. "Some of the smaller boats might get caught under the ice, but the middle of the creek will probably stay open all winter, and the larger ships will probably be able to still make it."

He paused, having thought it all out. "You could put the important messages in the big boats, the ones that you really wanted to get out, and the other, little, prettier messages, in the little boats, so if they got through in winter, well, all right, but if we didn't find them till spring, then that'd be all right, too — they'd fit in anywhere, being so pretty and all."

Jyl laughed. "All right," she said. "It sounds like a good plan." She invited them in, watched them stomp the snow from their boots and dust it from their arms and shoulders, helped them hang their coats and hats on the door hooks as if they were proper adults rather than children bearing adults' ways.

The pantry was almost empty — she'd been able to drink a little fruit juice, and sometimes to gnaw on an orange for strength, or, strangely, raisins, having begun to develop an affinity for them, if not a craving — and the children wanted none of these, but she was able to find a couple of old envelopes of instant oatmeal, as well as some equally ancient packages of hot chocolate mix.

They sat at the table, where Jyl had not had company in several months. She tried to remember the last company she'd had, and could not. The memory of it, the fact of it, seemed to get tangled in the snow falling outside the window, which they sat watching.

"Mama said to ask you how you're doing," Stephan said. "If you need anything. If there's anything we can do." He peered sidelong at Jyl, evaluating, she could tell, her girth, or gauntness, to take back home to tell his mother — glancing at her and making a reading or judgment as he would in a similar glance the health of a cow or horse, or even some wild creature in the woods, one he was perhaps considering taking. "She said to ask if you're eating yet." Another glance, as if he'd been warned that the interviewee might not be trusted to give direct or even truthful answers. "She said to ask if you needed any propane. If you needed any firewood.

If you needed any firewood split. If you needed any water hauled."

He said this last task so flatly, so casually and indifferently, that his practiced childish nonchalance illuminated rather than hid his distaste for the job, and again Jyl smiled, almost laughed, and said, "No, I don't need any water hauled, thank you — I've got a well and a pump" — and a look of pure desire crossed both children's faces.

"But you need some wood," Stephan said. A glance at the nearly empty wood box by the stove — only a few sticks of kindling. "Everybody always needs wood, and especially split wood." Another evaluation of her physique — the wasted arms, the pallor. The steady fright.

"Yes," Jyl admitted, "I could use some wood. And I've been wondering, too, what I'll do if I go out hunting, and do get an animal down. Before my illness — my cancer — I could just gut it and drag it home from wherever I'd shot it. But now it would take me so many trips that the ravens and eagles and coyotes would finish it off long before I ever got it all packed out."

Stephan nodded, as if the concern were music to his ears. "We can help with that," he said, and she saw that already his indoctrination was complete, that work had become his religion, that it transcended escape and was instead merely its own pure thing: that from early on, he and his brothers and sisters had been poured into the vessel of it, and it would be forever after how they were comfortable in the world. "We can take care of that," he said. "If you get an animal, you just let us know."

"Send us a note," Shayna said, again quiet and shy. Magic sparking in both of them like the tapping of flint against steel.

Stephan finished the rest of his hot chocolate in two gulps, then was up and headed for the door, with Shayna behind him like a shadow; and Jyl was surprised by the wrenching she felt in their sudden leave-taking.

She followed them out to the porch — they had already donned their coats and hats and were pulling on their gloves — and, slipping on her own snow gear, hurrying to keep them from waiting, she went out into the falling snow with them and down to her toolshed, where she showed them the saw, the cans of gas, the jug of bar oil. The battered wheelbarrow, unused since last summer.

"That rifle, back there on your porch," Stephan said. "It looked like an old one. Did it belong to your father, or your grandfather?"

"Yes," said Jyl. "My father's. I don't know where it came from before that — if it was his father's, or not."

Stephan was already sniffing the gas-and-oil mixture to see how old it was, and he looked up at Jyl as if this were the first thing she had said that had surprised him — as if he found such an admission unimaginable — and he said, "Are you a Christian?"

His expression was so earnest, his face so framed with concern, that again Jyl's first impulse was to laugh; but then her legs felt weak and the blood rushed from her head, so that she looked around quickly for a stump, and she took a seat and braced herself against the waves of dizziness, and the nausea. The snow was coming down harder: curtains and curtains of it.

"No, I don't guess I am," Jyl said. "I mean, I don't know: there's parts I believe, and parts that touch my heart" — she raised a gloved fist to her chest — "but the whole package . . .

I don't know." She looked up in the direction of the craggy mountain, invisible now in the falling snow. "I guess I find God more in the out-of-doors, and in the way we treat one another, than in any church. I've never cared to sit inside for anything unless I absolutely had to."

Stephan glanced over at Shayna with a look that Jyl could not identify, then hefted the chain saw and started up the hill toward a lichen-shrouded lodgepole. "You mind if we cut that one?" he asked, and Jyl smiled, shook her head, and said, "That was the one I was going to pick myself."

The saw had been idle for almost a year, and it took Stephan nearly ten minutes of cranking before it would even cough. During that time, Shayna and Jyl sat hunkered on their heels in the hard-falling snow, watching Stephan wrestle with the starter cord, panting and pausing to catch his wind — and from time to time he would look over at Jyl with the realization that not in a thousand years would she ever have been able to start the saw, in her weakened condition — and what would she have done then, with no wood? Driven into town and lived like a homeless person until the spring? Spent eight hours a day scrounging the snowy hills for damp twigs and branches? Attempted, in her puny shape, to gather her firewood with an ax?

The saw finally caught — went miraculously, suddenly, from a weak and faint sputter to full-throated burbling roar, complete with belch of blue smoke; and Stephan stood up straight, relief and pleasure on his face.

He moved to the tree and eased the spinning blade into the dead flesh — white chips flew like rice at a wedding — and cut a notch, which he slid out of the tree expertly, and then he went around to the other side and made the back cut. And as if following the bidding of some master anti-architect, in which there was as much grace in the laying down as in the building up, the tree eased itself gracefully down the hill, falling slowly through the swirling snow in such a manner as to disorient all three of them.

The tree bounced when it hit, and the dry branches snapped and popped and went flying in all directions; and even before the sifting clouds of snow stirred up by its impact had drifted away, Shayna had risen and was moving alongside the fallen tree, gathering those small branches in her arms, gathering a double armful, as many as she could carry, and taking them to the porch, some fifty yards distant, trudging through snow that was now over her knees.

Jyl watched and tried to remember her own childhood, and wondered if childhood felt to Shayna as it once had to her, when she had been so small — as if sometimes the world was filling with snow and trying to bury her.

Stephan was moving quickly along the fallen tree, bucking it up, severing more limbs, and Jyl went out to help him, began gathering her own armfuls of limbs and branches, and started carrying them back to her porch, following the initial trail that Shayna had blazed in the snow.

They smiled at each other in passing, Shayna returning with arms empty for another load, and Jyl struggling, with hers full; and now Stephan had the log completely delimbed and was cutting it into firewood, spacing his quick and neat cuts in metronomic sixteen-inch spacings that seemed as precise as the mechanical bobbings of a water ouzel perched on a streamside boulder, crouching and dipping ceaselessly: always the same distance, always the same motion, like a wind-up toy.

It was not a very big tree, and they had it entirely dismembered, split and hauled and stacked, within a half-hour: a porch full of bright, gleaming new-cut firewood, and a fresh-lumber scent dense upon them, like the odor of new beginnings, and possibility.

They went inside to dust off for a moment, to wash the scent of oil smoke from their faces and to pour a glass of water. The darkness was coming quickly.

"We'll be back tomorrow to get some more," Stephan said. "Or as soon as we can. And to do other things."

"Listen," said Jyl, "I know how busy you all are. I know how much you all have to do at home. This is more than enough. I'll be fine, really. It's so kind of you to do even this. I'll be fine. Thank you. Tell your mother thank you."

"We can't keep a regular schedule," Stephan said. "There's too much to do at home. We can just come when we get our chores done."

"I'm here in the evenings," Jyl said. "Mornings, I'm almost always sleeping. After lunch, I go get my treatment. But I'm here at night."

"When do you sail the boats?" Shayna asked, her voice little more than a whisper, like the stirring of a bird back in the brush. More of a fluttering than a voice.

"Afternoons," Jyl said, "when I get back from the hospital, and just before I go in to nap."

"We usually get them right before suppertime," she said.

"I'll send one tomorrow," Jyl said. "I'll send two, a big boat and a little boat, each with the same message, so that if one gets hung up the other one might still make it through."

"Oh, no," Shayna said quickly, surprising Jyl with her assertiveness. "If you send two you can write different messages, because we'll find them both. We'll go upstream looking for them. We'll find them."

"Is that what you've been doing with these?" Jyl asked. "If one doesn't come by your house, you go upstream, searching for it?"

Shayna nodded. "He takes one side and I take the other. It's fun. We go after chores, and after supper. Sometimes we go at night, and use lanterns."

"Do you ever worry that one gets past you — that you never see it?"

The children looked at each other. "We all keep a pretty good eye out for them, most of the day," Stephan said. He paused. "Some of the kids wanted to put a fishnet across the creek, and check it regular, but Shayna and I didn't want to do it that way."

"It's okay if there's days you can't send one," Shayna said. "We know you're busy, and that there's days you have to rest."

Jyl smiled. "I'm getting better," she said. "I can't make any promises, but it's good to know the ships are getting through."

The snow was still falling hard, and although such a heavy snowfall so early in the year assured them of a long winter, it also meant a reduced fire season, next summer; knowing this, they accepted both the hardship and the blessing of it with neither praise nor complaint, and instead only watched it, as animals might.

"Do you need another flashlight?" Jyl asked. "Or do you want to stay here for the night?"

The children looked horrified at the latter suggestion. "We've got to be up early," Stephan explained.

"How early?"

"Four," he said.

It was almost dusk. Jyl could smell the chain saw odor on them and wondered if they would bathe when they got home or simply crawl into their sleeping bags in the warm loft, surrounded by the breathing sounds of their sleeping siblings and the occasional stove creak of one of their parents adding wood to the fire downstairs, and the compressed hush of the snow falling on the roof, just inches away from their faces as they slept warm in that loft.

"Thank you," she told them as they set off into the gloom, with Stephan breaking trail for his sister.

After their light had disappeared, she put on her heavy coat and gloves and got her father's rifle and went into the woods a short distance, and sat down beneath the embrace of a big spruce tree, and waited a few moments to settle in — to adjust her heart, pounding from even that small exertion, to the space and silence around her. She took off her gloves and blew through cupped hands.

She put her gloves back on, lifted her rifle, and waited, then, listening to the falling snow. It was right at the edge of being too dark to shoot. She could hear the creek riffling behind her, and she listened to that for a while, lulled. Her cabin, not a hundred yards distant, beckoned, as did her warm bed — for a moment her mind strayed ahead to the relief, the dull harbor, she found in sleep each night — and she began to feel ridiculous, tucked in so invisible against the world, as if in a burrow; as if she were hiding in the one place where no one could ever find her, the one place where she was least likely to find her quarry.

She was settling into a reverie, had already given up the notion of hunting and was instead merely dreaming, when there came slowly into her consciousness a sound that was unlike the other sounds and silences that had been surrounding her: a jarring, clumsy sound of eagerness, hoofs slipping on wet rocks, a clattering and splashing, then silence again.

She sat up and peered through her lattice of branches. She heard the sound of quiet steps approaching, but then the steps ceased. She waited for five minutes, ears and eyes straining — she tried to catch the scent of the animal but could smell nothing, only wet falling snow — and then she heard the animal crossing back over the creek, going away; and when she rose stiffly from her crouch, her warren beneath the tree, and went to examine the tracks, they were already filled in with new snow, and it was as if the thing had never existed.

When she got back to her cabin and its warmth and yellow light, she was surprised by how late it was — by how she had confused the soft blue luminous light cast by the snow with the fading light of dusk. It was nearly seven o'clock, and she was cold, wet, and shivering.

She was still stimulated by the hunt, and by the children's visit, and would have liked to have stayed up late, or even until a normal hour — taking a leisurely hot bath and curling up in bed afterward, and reading until midnight, as she had once done in the freedom of her health.

But she had extended herself too far, that day, and in the end she simply sat by the wood stove, shivering, and feeding it more wood. One of the propane lanterns in that corner of the cabin sputtered and coughed into darkness, leaving only one remaining lamp hissing over on the far side of the cabin; and though the silence was still lonelier, in the subdued lighting, she took a short fragment of firewood from the wood box and got out her pocketknife and tried to begin carving a new toy ship.

She had not carved more than three minutes, however, before fatigue overtook her — not so much physical exhaustion or the brutishness of fear, but instead the cumulative fatigue of loneliness combining with all those other exhaustions — *five percent chance of survival,* the doctors had told her, *five percent, five percent* — and yet somehow, frugal and efficient to her core, she managed to rouse and walk the ten paces over to the other side of the cabin and turn off the lone remaining lamp.

She was chilled immediately, however, away from the stove, and so she pulled a quilt off her bed and went back over to the fire, stoked it up again, and, too tired to even change out of her damp clothes, curled up against the stove's base, wrapped herself tightly in the quilt, and fell asleep there on the floor, with no padding, no comfort, no thoughts, no anything, only falling; and with the pocketknife still open beside her, and the block of wood with less than a handful of shavings carved off beside it: not even enough shavings to kindle the smallest of fires.

Despite the depth of her fatigue, she dreamed: as if the mind or spirit requires no energy, or, rather, feeds from some source other than the body, flowing almost continuously.

She dreamed of traveling her mountain again: of traversing it that night, at times following the same trail the children had made going home, and other times making her own. In the dream, it was still snowing, and the snow was over her knees, as it was in the real life just outside her door; and there was something about the dream, some synchronized in-the-moment aspect to it, that made it seem extraordinarily real, vibrant, and refreshing. It was almost as if her spirit was trying to heal or repair itself, even where her body could not or had not yet; almost as if so severe was the damage to one, the body or vessel of her, that that other current, sometimes separate and other times twined, was becoming also abraded. And as if it would do whatever was necessary, for the healing.

She moved with strength and steadiness up the trail. It was not easy going, but the labor felt good. The snow was falling on her face, and though she was wearing a heavy coat and gloves and gaiters, her head was bare, and at times she would stop and shake the snow from her hair.

She ascended steadily. Even though she was only walking, time seemed to pass more quickly than it ever had — as if an hour were now only a second — and in no time at all she was back on the ledge that ran along the high cliff of the mountain's west face.

And looking down through the slanting snow, and down through the snow-shrouded canopy of the dense forest so far below, she could see lights moving like fireflies, a handful of lanterns scattered through the forest and along the river, some coming and others going.

The lights looked like the flares from torches, or drifting sparks from a campfire, or scattered little wildfires seen on distant mountains at night in the autumn; but the slow carriage of them was distinctly that of humans, on foot.

At first Jyl thought the lantern carriers were searching for something; but, pausing to watch the course and pacing of their lights, she understood quickly that they were engaged in some sort of labor, and, as she stood there a while longer, with the snow piling up on her back and shoulders, the picture became even clearer for her, and she understood that it was the children, passing back and forth through the woods, carrying buckets of water for the family's baths, the family's cooking, and the family's drinking.

The loaded-bucket travelers moved slowly, on their way back from the river to the cabin, the lights of which were not visible — perhaps extinguished for economy at that hour. The empty-bucket travelers, going from the cabin back down to the river, moved faster while passing through those same woods, and when one of the going-away lanterns passed one of the coming-up lanterns, there was no pause — each kept traveling in its own direction — and though Jyl had no real way of knowing, it seemed to her that in such weather and amid such weariness, and at so late an hour, no words were passed between the travelers.

Jyl remained standing, watching, as if turned to a statue. The snow kept piling up on and around her, and after a while — long hours, perhaps, though in the dream it seemed like only moments — the procession ceased, the water tanks had all been filled.

The lanterns all assembled in one place on the front porch, and then one by one they blinked out, until only two were remaining.

These two did not blink out, but instead turned and moved slowly back into the forest, again barely visible through the falling snow — disappearing, at times, beneath its burden, as if having been submerged briefly before reappearing a little farther into the forest.

The river, though not visible, was identifiable as a wandering line between darkness and light, an imaginary border in the forest, at which all the lanterns had previously paused at the end of their bucket-filling marches.

Jyl watched now as one of the lanterns went slightly farther than any of the others had — the traveler, either Shayna or Stephan, crossing snow-covered mossy stones to stay dry.

Both lights turned then and began following the invisible trace of the river upstream, the banks and borders defined and limned by that wavering, snow-blinking campfire light, as if the river were embedded in ice and it was the lanterns' path that was cutting it free of the ice, releasing it and allowing it to flow again.

And it was a helpless feeling for Jyl, being up there on the mountain, on the cliff, knowing she had not sent out a vessel that day, or a message, a missive, no little painting or inscription.

She tried her best to call down to the searchers, but the words seemed lost even before she uttered them, as if all the world was snow and as if speech were a phenomenon that could not exist in this dream-world — and so she tried to will the children to turn around and give up, not to waste their time; though still they came on, moving slowly, one on either side of the river, stopping and starting, and searching: lifting up fallen logs, she supposed, and peering carefully into riffles and eddies, hoping and searching.

And in the dream, it was too sad to watch, and Jyl was eager to be moving again, eager to be on her mountain again, having had her strength and energy restored to her, even if only for the evening; and so, reluctantly, the statue of her melted, turned from its frozen position, shedding that thick mantling of snow, and hurried on farther up the mountain to the top, pushing on through the knee-deep and then thigh-deep snow like a plow horse, on past the faint and lost-looking smatterings of light so far below and on up to the mountaintop where she had been so many times before — a place she had previously taken for granted, but which she did not that evening, in the dream.

Instead, she lay spread-eagled on its top, face upturned to

the whirling, sifting snow, and, in its embrace, she slept: just for a little while, just long enough to grow warm, just long enough to remember, and savor, what it had been like to be healthy.

And in the dream she did not have to descend, did not have to pass back by the searchers, but instead woke at daylight by her cold extinguished wood stove, her breath frosty in her own cabin.

She poured a glass of water for breakfast. She ate two crackers, which was two more than she had the stomach for. She built the fire back up and sat beside it and resumed whittling, falling asleep sometimes with the knife still in her hand, and her head leaning against the cabin wall, only to jerk awake again, having returned in her nap to the mountaintop, and with too much snow atop her now — having slept too long.

What story to tell them, in the little bottles? Was her own childhood of any importance to them, or was it better to help them create their own?

Should she tell them, for instance, that her father, a bush pilot, had invented a system for mechanically retrieving rock samples from the sides of mountains by using a dangling claw hook, like a backhoe's digging bucket, which trailed below the plane like a kite tail and snatched at the side of the mountain, gouging and clawing at it, as he flew past — jarring the plane terribly, but managing to grab, in that manner, a bucketful of stone, in country that might otherwise have taken weeks to get to on foot? Or similarly dredging the bottom of an alluvial riverbed?

Should she tell them that he helped pioneer a methodology of analyzing the tops of trees — isolating and identifying by chemical analysis the minerals present in the green needles and leaves — and from those assays he fashioned then a map of the mineral content of the subsurface formations below, as if the spires of the trees were but extensions of those rocks, those minerals — still fixed in place, but born now into towering life?

He would fly over vast stretches of forest, lowering his claw-bucket sample-chopper, and would snatch up one tree-top after another, would reel it up like a fishing line, flying the plane with one hand and running the crank with his other; and in this manner he covered thousands of square miles more effectively than entire squadrons of geologists could have done, achieving in a single field season that which might have taken less daring or driven geologists a lifetime to accomplish.

Should she tell them that many days she considered being — desired to be — a mother?

Or should she tell them fairy tales — stories of princes and princesses of extraordinary power and purity, powerful beings unhindered by flaw or imperfection — durable, enduring, even immortal? Myths and tales toward which the children could move, as if sighting a light, a lantern lit in the night, not too far ahead of them?

Still frightened of the past, she chose the latter. She kept her father's stories within her ill-wracked body, and even her own stories, and instead worked on a story about a prince and princess.

In the story, the ruler of the boy and girl's country, a kind and wise king, is washed over a waterfall while trying to save a small girl in distress, a girl caught out in the rapids; though the child is saved, the great king is swept over the falls and broken into pieces below, with his parts carried downstream for miles.

Over the years, the great king's parts — head, arms, legs, feet, hands, back, chest — wash up on shore from time to time and become hardened into stone, or driftwood; and walking along the river, the prince and princess occasionally come across his remnants, and they gather them up to take back home.

Slowly, over the years, they collect enough pieces to begin reassembling the great king, and one day they come to understand, or believe, that if they can fully reassemble him he will come back to life, in all his previous goodness and fullness and glory and power.

But the boy and girl are growing up now, and soon it will be time for them to assume the responsibility of becoming the leaders of their country; and as they find more and more body parts of the old king — a finger, a foot, a nose, an ear — they are hesitant to finish putting him back together, hesitant to bring him back to life.

Still, they cannot stop searching. Each day they walk along the river, looking, and they search at night, too, with lanterns: for sometimes there are parts of the old king that emerge from the depths, from beneath the gravel and silt, under the pull of the moon. Sometimes a muscled driftwood arm will float in the night in the dark waters, glinting beneath that moonlight, only to sink again at dawn; and the children, nearly grown now, continue searching, but cannot decide whether to complete their search or to finally turn away from it and travel on into the future, leaving the broken parts behind.

The tedium of her days, the tedium of her new life: for a long time it had been getting harder and harder for her to summon the strength to get in the truck and haul herself to town for the treatments. She thought she might be getting better, though, when the fatigue began to give way to boredom. It wasn't a regular boredom, but was instead so overbearing as to masquerade at first as continued fatigue. Slowly, however, she came to realize the subtle difference — the subtle improvement. The cancer was gone, and her normal cells, with their normal mandates, were returning slowly, whirling and dancing and executing their ancient motions of electrolysis, glycogen transfer, oxygenation, and tissue repair — and even as the darkness of winter fell over the land, she could feel faintly the dynamics of light returning cautiously to the fragile, fire-bombed husk of her body.

She continued to carve her ships in the waiting room, where the doctors, nurses, and other patients were amazed by them. She sanded and polished their bows and hulls of pinewood until they were as smooth as eggs. She wrote each day's sentence in a careful script of calligraphy, watercolored each illustration, and launched the ship each afternoon upon returning home from the treatment.

There was no way for her to visit the Workmans. They lived in the secluded little valley that was on the other side of the mountain, on an old mining homestead. They kept their truck parked out on the nearest road, it would be farther for her to walk in that way than it would be for her to cross over the ponderous mountain. They had no mail service, no phone. The ships were the only way in.

Upon returning home from her treatments she would nap, and then rouse herself at dusk and go out into the woods with her rifle. The deer were more active now, with the rut ongoing, and with the deepening snow forcing them to travel almost constantly, searching for food, using the trails they had cut through the snow, used over and over again, becoming almost pedestrian in their regularity — but still she was not seeing any.

Sometimes she would hear their feet crunching lightly through the snow and ice, and sometimes she would even catch a glimpse of a dull silhouette of a deer as it was already turning away, having sighted or scented her just before she noticed it. Sometimes she would even see a glint of antler; and in the leap of adrenaline, the bolt of excitement that rushed upward in her like fire at such a sight, she knew more than ever that she was getting better: but still, the deer would not let her have them.

Her father had been gone twenty years now. Her father had never known her diminished. Were she and he like two different mountains, she wondered, slightly different kinds of stone through which the same river of time ran, or were they like two braids or forks of a river separating — running across, and cutting down into, the same one mountain, the same one face and body of stone?

And what if we had it all backwards, she wondered. What if it is the mountain and the past that are living, while the river and the present are the unliving: merely a physical force, like wind, or electricity, but not really alive, not in the sense that blood or memory is alive?

It was nonsense, she knew. Of course rivers were alive. Of course mountains and stones were alive. And of course the world possessed an invisible topography of spirit, with ridges, valleys, glaciers, volcanoes, tides and creeks and bays and oceans of spirit, and with as many different carriers of spirit, in that invisible world, the world of the past, as there were carriers of life in the visible, tangible, physical world:

elk, bison, man, woman, child, antelope, deer, bear, tree, bird...

Her father had collected fossils and gemstones — tourmaline, topaz, opal, jade, malachite, amethyst — and upon his death, she had carted all the various shoeboxes of minerals back to her home, where she kept them stored in the basement.

And, believing now that her stories and illustrations were no longer sufficient to summon the children, she began putting little gems and crystals in the ships. As if laying treasures before young kings and queens.

Whom should she serve — the future, or the past? How much time did she have left to serve? What value was any mineral, any fossil, compared to the spark of life? She felt guilty, releasing some of her father's finer treasures, but each day she filled the boats higher and higher with glittering bounty.

It was nearly a week before Stephan and Shayna returned. They came on the weekend before Thanksgiving.

She was out hunting again, or if not actually hunting, then sitting with her back propped against a spruce tree, beneath the protection of its branches, watching the snow, mesmerized by the snow, and waiting for a deer to perhaps walk past.

When she heard the children's voices coming over the mountain, she did not understand at first that they were coming her way, coming to visit her, but that instead she was dreaming again, and was traveling to go see them, to meet them in their little valley, and that as she drew closer she was now able to hear them more clearly. And when she saw them appear from out of the woods, barely visible at first in the falling snow, her first thought was that they were wolves, or even bears. There was something about their movements that did not make her think of people.

Even as they crossed the creek, stepping carefully from stone to stone, trying to stay dry, they did not appear through that screen of falling snow to be fully human; and when she saw that they each carried in their arms burlap sacks filled with something, still they did not remind her of her own kind; and while the drift of their voices, more audible now, was clearly the sound of children, their conversation did not seem to be connected to the two figures she saw tiptoeing across the river.

She unchambered her rifle and rose to greet them — they were already knocking on her door, calling her name, and, not hearing a response, going into the cabin anyway — and as she moved toward them through the snow and darkness, there seemed to be little difference between how she felt now and how she had felt in her earlier dream of ascending the mountain and looking down upon their wandering lights; though she was aware, tripping and stumbling a bit, of a palpitation of her heart, and an overarching eagerness, that had not been present in the dream.

She had been leaving one lantern burning low each night, in case they should come then — in the hopes that they would come, so that they, too, would be able to look down from the mountain through the falling snow and see her own light, visible in the storm, and home in on it, not so much as if lost but instead sighting finally the thing they had been searching for.

As she approached her own cabin now, she saw the lantern flare more brightly — illuminating the thousands of individual snowflakes floating past the windows — and she felt safe, and as if life had not yet even called out to her, as if her life had not yet even begun.

She saw them moving around inside the yellowing dome of light, talking to one another and looking up at the books on her shelves; and when she stomped the snow from her boots and went on inside, still wet and snowy from her vigil beneath the spruce, she was warmed by the relief on the boy's face, and by the joy on the girl's.

"Did you see any deer?" Stephan asked, straight away.

She shook her head, hugged them — they seemed glad to receive the hugs — and shook her head again. "I think they can smell my illness," she said. "I can hear and sometimes see them coming closer, but at the last minute they turn away."

Stephan sniffed the air. "I can't smell it," he said, "and usually I can smell anything."

Jyl shrugged. "It's there," she said. "Even I can smell it."

"What does it smell like?" Shayna asked.

"Metal," Jyl said, pouring water into the cast-iron kettle and setting it on the stove, then opening the stove and stoking in some more kindling, which the dull-glowing coals accepted and ignited quickly. "I don't know. Steel, platinum, copper, gold, silver. Some kind of cold metal," she said. She waggled her jaws as if to rid herself of the taste of it.

"Is it on your breath?" she asked. "Do you think we could try to smell it?"

Jyl covered her mouth involuntarily and turned away. "No," she said. "I don't want you to smell it."

They were quiet for a while, after that. Finally Stephan

said, "We really can't smell anything. But if you think the deer can, maybe you should try and mask it. Maybe you should have a piece of peppermint or licorice before you go out next time. Maybe they'll be curious and come a little closer. Maybe they'll think it's another animal."

She had restocked her pantry, hoping that the children would come again — had bought far too much food, beyond her budget, and not knowing what they liked and did not like, had guessed — some sugary cereals, a kind of frozen Popsicle treat, some TV dinners of mashed potatoes and cod; apples, oranges, bananas; some frozen salmon filets, Canadian bacon, a frozen pizza, and a frozen strawberry cheesecake — and when she asked what they wanted for supper they told her they usually had rice and pineapple, and that was about all they liked — rice and pineapple, and venison and elk.

She felt a despair, a failure that she had not known since the hardest days of her treatment. She was surprised by the tears that leapt to her eyes, and she turned quickly to where they could not see them. When she had composed herself, she asked, "Would you eat a cheesecake?"

They nodded solemnly, as if it were a trick question, and Stephan said, "We'll eat anything — it's just that we only like rice and pineapple and elk and venison." They were surprised, then, she could tell — almost spooked — by her wild laughter.

She set about preparing the salmon, thawing it out in warm water. She cut the cheesecake into little wedges and served it to them first, and put a couple of the TV dinners in the stove as well, in the hopes they might find something to pick at. She needn't have worried, for soon they were asking for more of the cheesecake, and she even had a piece, and then had to put the rest out on the porch or they might have eaten it all.

"It'll refreeze," she said cunningly. "You can have the rest of it the next time you come."

She put the salmon in the oven with the TV dinners, braised it with butter and garlic and lemon and orange, then sat down by the stove and took the bolt from her rifle and began cleaning and oiling it, while they sat at the table next to her and ate the cheesecake and drank hot chocolate. When she was done she put the rifle back together and hung it up in the snow room, and changed into dry clothes.

She could tell that although the children were still cold and weary, they were uncomfortable simply relaxing, and were anxious to be leaving. She sought to detain them with stories and knowledge. She walked over to a bookshelf and pulled down one of her father's old texts, *Ancient Sedimentary Environments*, published in 1940. Dust motes rose from it as she opened its covers; and from across the room, still eating the cheesecake, both Stephan and Shayna sniffed the air, and Stephan said, "I can smell that."

"It's got pictures," Jyl said, bringing it over to the table. She thumbed through the pages, and her eyes blurred as she read for the first time some of the markings he had underlined in pencil a lifetime ago.

"The consensus of geological opinion is that there are a finite number of sedimentary facies which occur repeatedly in rocks of different ages all over the world. Therefore, no two similar sedimentary facies are ever identical, and gradational transitions are common.

"One of the main problems of determining the origin of ancient sediments is that, though essentially reflecting depositional environments, they also inherit features of earlier environment. The infilled sediment reflects the nature of the source rocks and the hydraulic of the current, while the rolled bones and wood and other fossiliferous inclusions are derived from non-depositional environments that lie for the most part beyond the stream's usual reach. No rock is ever finished, all stones are continually being remade, until they vanish from the face of the earth. And yet, even then, once reduced to windblown dust, they are reforming."

The children had stopped eating, their forks in midair, and were listening, though Stephan was slowly raising his hand in what was unmistakably mild protest. Jyl could tell also that they were suspicious, as if they understood somehow that their fundamentalist faith might be challenged by such language. Still, she read on:

"A classic example of this fallacy can be found in a profile of the Bu Hasa Rudist boundstones, which pass basinward into skeletal wackestones, with fragments of rudists and large benthonic Orbitoline forams. These wackestones pass basinward into lime mudstones. The rudist boundstone passes south towards the Arabian shield into faccal pellet muds, with miliolid foraminifera. Locally however the basinward crest of the rudist boundstone is replaced by a detrital rudist grainstone."

There was a look very close to despair on Stephan's face — Shayna showed no such distress and was instead only staring at Jyl with utter wonder — but Jyl could see that Stephan wasn't going to give up or back away; and with his brows furrowed, he reached for a pencil and paper on the table and asked carefully, slowly, "What's rudist?"

She couldn't hold back her laughter, then — it spilled from her again, clean and clear, with a feeling of release that she could not remember knowing before, and she said, "I don't know."

Stephan took the book from her and looked through it, at all the many such passages underlined in long-ago pencil. "But he knew all this stuff, right?" he asked. "Your father knew all this?"

Jyl nodded, her eyes stinging with pride.

"I'd like to read this book," Stephan said. "I know it means a lot to you, and I wouldn't ask to take it with me — I wouldn't want to get it banged up — but I'd like to read it, and make notes from it, while I'm over here."

Jyl smiled. "All right. But let's start over. Let's start at the beginning." She took down a roll of butcher paper, spread it across the table, and began with the basics, explaining the different ways rocks can be formed from the ash and guts and detritus of the earth: the igneous rocks arising straight from the cooling fire of subterranean cauldrons, the sedimentary rocks the cumulative residue of dust and grit and silt being deposited with the earnestness of a mason, the sediments not settling by fiery will, but obedient instead only to the inescapable mandates of gravity; and the metamorphic rocks, her favorites: stones so substantially altered from their original igneous or sedimentary form by the world's and time's terrible pressures, smoothed now into graceful curves and folded into fantastic swirls and reversals, so that the geologist examining them could sometimes not tell at first in which direction the past ran and in which, the future . . .

As she talked, she illustrated her lecture with watercolors, sketching mountains and oceans, rivers and storms, showing how the simple forces of weather — morning sunrise, wind, frost, snow and rain — in conjunction with the earth's own subtle movements, its faint stretches and belches and yawns, conspire across the arc of time to wear even the largest and most jagged mountains down to desert plains, and how even the oceans fall back to reveal their gleaming, glittering mud, which is then lifted miles into the sky, creeping upward a thousandth of an inch per year, but leaping nonetheless, and carrying in that hardened crypt many of the fossils that had once lived far beneath the sea, and which would now be spending eons so much closer to the sun, suspended atop mountains, exposed to wind and rain and snow, the hoofs of mountain goats, and the curious eyes of man, and all the glittering green world shining below . . .

With her sketches, she detailed the creation of alluvial fans, longshore point bars, tectonic plates, and unconformities. The world-beneath-the-world, the stone world on the back of which rested the living world, was born for the children that night, and they began to understand that it, too, was living, though at a different pace, and that although such knowledge might trouble their parents' beliefs, they were riding on the earth's back, and that beneath the stone world there was even another, third world, on the back of which the stone world rode, and that that third and even lower world was the river or current of time . . .

Jyl had started painting the cross sections of geological time for them, starting at the surface and intending to work all the way down, through the dinosauric creations and into the world-flooded Devonian and Silurian, into the stone-cold Cambrian, and then farther, into the colder, utterly lifeless time of Precambrian, but Shayna reminded her of the salmon and the TV dinners in the oven, and Jyl looked up in total surprise, having been so immersed in the teaching, and so unaccustomed to cooking, that she only vaguely remembered having put the food in the oven; and setting her paintbrush down and hurrying over to the stove, she found that the big salmon was perfect, though the TV dinners were a little crispy.

They suspended their geology lecture for the evening and sat around the fireplace and ate their dinners. Jyl told them about her time in Alaska, and about a pilot she had known there, a young man who had flown her around in a floatplane to much of the same backcountry where her father had worked: visiting the same lakes and walking along the same beaches, looking at the same mountains. It was this same pilot who had sent her the salmon they were eating, and she told them that when she got better she had it in her mind to go back up there and visit him.

"Will you marry him?" Shayna asked. A fairy tale.

Jyl laughed. "No," she said, "he's just a friend. Just a bush pilot. But I like his company."

"We were in Alaska," Stephan said. "Just before she was born."

"Where?" Jyl said. "Doing what?"

"Missionary stuff. We were in Seward, but Pa would fly into the villages a lot. I'm pretty sure it was missionary stuff."

"How long were you there?"

Stephan shrugged. "Just a couple of years. Mama didn't like it. Nobody liked it. It was beautiful, but nobody liked it."

They were all quiet for a while, before Shayna finally said, quietly — as if in Jyl's defense, or defense of Jyl's father — "I would have liked it."

Jyl smiled. "So y'all like it here?"

Stephan shrugged. "I think so," he said. "Sometimes it's a little hard — the work — but I think so."

"I do," said Shayna. "I love it."

It was past nine o'clock — the latest Jyl had stayed up since before the illness. She took down some old elk hides from her closet and prepared twin pallets for the children next to the wood stove, and then, feeling her weariness returning like the break of a towering wave, she barely had time and energy to clean the dishes before collapsing into her own bed. She was asleep even before the children were, even as the children were still visiting with her quietly, talking between themselves and asking her occasional questions: and when they realized she was asleep, Stephan got up and wrote his questions down on the butcher paper with its illustrations so that he would not forget them. Questions about different minerals, and different kinds of salmon; about the floatplane, and about her father.

Then he turned out the lantern, and he and Shayna, though restless in the new surroundings, tried to get to sleep as quickly as possible, knowing that they would need to conserve their strength for the trip home and the coming day. The unfamiliar stove burned its wood differently, made different sounds, and through the glass plate in its door they could see the sparks and embers swirling and glowing, and they stared at it as if viewing the maw of a tiny volcano.

The children slept until two, when they awakened to a fire that was nearly out — quietly, Stephan built it back up — and they dressed warmly and went out into the night to fell another tree for Jyl before leaving.

The storm had passed, leaving a crystalline glaze over the world as the temperatures fell, and the snowflakes, quick-frozen now, tinkled like glass scales as they passed through them. Their breath rose in jets of fog when they spoke, and when they came to the next dead pine, Stephan started the saw, felled the tree and bucked it as fast as possible, not wanting to awaken Jyl, and then shut the saw off and let the huge silence of the stars sweep back in over them.

Because the snow was deep, it took them more than an hour to split and carry that wood to the porch, stacking it as quietly as possible; and by the time they had the saw and maul and gas and oil cans stored, and the bark and snow swept from the porch, they were later getting away than they had intended, so that they had to run, galloping through the snow like draft horses, and steaming from their effort.

They made it back to their cabin — exhausted, but arrived — and quietly there, too, set about their labors in preparation for the day.

Jyl dreamed again that she was running, though with difficulty this time rather than in the effortless glide of the previous dream. And there was a pain in her gut as her glycogen-depleted organs cramped and sought to metabolize her muscle and bone, and even themselves — metabolizing anything for just a bit more available energy, in order to keep going, to keep struggling up the hill.

It was a sensation she recognized from her earlier days of strength, when she had been able to run seemingly without ceasing; and in the dream, though it was painful, she welcomed it, glad as she was to be back on the mountain.

Finally, though, the pain awakened her, and she sat up, trying to be as quiet as possible to avoid waking the children. When she went to get a glass of water, she saw that they were gone; lighting a lantern to see if they had left a note, she found none, though she did see the questions Stephan had written down on the butcher paper in the middle of the night. And the sense of loss she knew was sharper than any stitch in her side, far deeper than any absence of glycogen.

Unable to get back to sleep, she built the fire up again and fixed a cup of tea, and set about answering their questions, writing the answers in the tiniest of script so that she could scroll them up into some of the larger message bottles and place them in one of the larger crafts, to set sail later that afternoon. Her answers would be a departure, a break, from the saga of the broken king, but one she welcomed; and as she worked on her notes — feeling as she had in college, laboring over an exam in which the correct answers were of utmost importance — she had the feeling also of being lured up from out of the depths and the darkness, and out into the bright light of some open and verdant spring meadow: as if she, and not her father, was the broken king, but that she was daring now, or at least desiring, to be reassembled.

It was almost dawn when she finished her answers. Though she knew she should go back to sleep, she was surprisingly restless, and the idea of going out to hunt a deer came to her so strongly that it was like a summons. She rose and began dressing warmly, and took her rifle down from its rack and loaded it, and went out into the darkness, past the scent of all the newly stacked firewood — she paused, and then, following the children's tracks, went into the woods, to the new stump.

It was almost daylight. The tops of her ears were cold, and she snuggled in tight against another big spruce, hid herself close among its lower branches, digging a little snow hollow in which to sit, and waited.

When it was light enough to see the shapes of things, the outlines of the trees coming into focus, she squinted and listened even more intently.

From across the river there came a crashing of sticks and branches so close and severe that she did not believe the sound could be made by any animal as graceful and stealthy as a deer but instead that it was Stephan and Shayna — that they were still back in the forest, searching for more firewood — and she was tempted to call out to them.

She remained silent, however, and the crashing came once more, followed by a silence, and then a splashing.

She leaned forward, trying with all her strength to see through the gray and barely penetrable light; and, as if sensing the acuity of her attention, the deer stopped midstream, just beyond her sight, and waited, weighing the danger, the hunger the deer could feel thick and living in the birth of the morning.

And as he stood there, water riffling around his ankles (Jyl could hear the different sound in it, the variance in splashing river rhythm as it braided around and past his four planted legs), the gray light grew more diffuse beneath the coming power of the day, and she was able finally to see the shape of him: his bulk, and the rack of his antlers so startling that it seemed he must surely be carrying in the nest of them a tangled mass of branches from farther back in the forest.

Before the excitement hit her, and the trembling, she had the thought, for half a second, that he, too, like the children, was bringing her firewood: that he was delivering it to her in his antlers.

As the light grew steadily stronger and more detail was revealed, she saw that the cluster of his antlers was all his, all hardened bone — and he stood there as motionless as a garden statue. Only his eyes showed life, and though it seemed he was looking straight at her, and had spied her hiding back in the branches, he finally moved again, emerging from whatever stony reverie he'd been in, and began walking toward her.

He reached her side of the river and stepped out, dripping.

He paused again, as if he had forgotten where he was. He seemed to enter another reverie, and as she watched him at this closer range she could see the old scars around his face from ancient battles, could see the clouds of breath coming from his nostrils, the old buck breathing hard from even such a mild exertion as the river crossing.

He appeared to be in some slightly other universe, some slightly different level or plane, suffused with grace and confidence even in his senescence. She imagined she could see doubt or anxiety trying to enter the buck's gaze, and his suspicion that something was wrong — and for a moment Jyl was overwhelmed with a feeling of unworthiness at being so close to such a wild creature, much less to be on the verge of taking his life.

The buck stepped out of his trance once more, reentered the world. He turned away from Jyl now and began walking along the trough made in the snow where Stephan and Shayna had felled their second tree. He stepped carefully over and among the tangle of branches Stephan had limbed from the tree, then lowered his head to browse on the lichen that clung to those branches; and each time he did so, Jyl felt a moment of disorientation as the crown of antlers lowered — as if a large bush was attached to the deer's head and beginning to move in animal fashion.

She was so amazed by the grace, the elegance, of the old deer's movements — his careful steps through and over the latticework of torn and sawn limbs — that she forgot she was hunting him. She watched as he lifted his head occasionally to glance around, and then lowered it to the snow and sniffed like a hound at the children's tracks.

Several times the deer stared off in the direction of her cabin, and Jyl had the feeling that the deer believed that he was safe, that he was secure in the faith that Jyl was still in her cabin, asleep. She could easily raise her rifle and drop him where he stood, while he stared as if transfixed at the yellow squares of her cabin — and yet something within her, some place of warmth, dissuaded her from making the shot, and instead she simply watched him watch her cabin.

After a while, then, he lowered his head to browse again, and drifted on farther into the woods, and though she wanted a deer, she was glad she had not taken this one, even though she knew she might not get another chance.

She had only one more week left of treatment. Millions of patients had been through it before — they would nearly all call it the most physically grueling and spiritual thing they'd ever done, and would often speak of the hidden blessing of the cancer, of the way it awakened in them incredible awareness of even the simplest pleasures. But such testimonials irked Jyl, for she did not feel she had ever taken those little moments for granted in the first place. On the contrary, she had always been acutely aware of them, even worshipful of them. It wasn't fair.

The treatment had been calibrated to reach its toxic peak during its last week, but she felt in every way that she had already turned the corner, that the worst week was just behind her, and that despite the increasing radioactive and chemical bombardment her body was growing stronger again. And when she told the doctors this, they shrugged and said that it was possible, that different patients responded in different ways.

She sent forth another boat, relating her saga of having seen the big deer, and inviting the children to return when they could. She told them she looked forward to it, and that she would bake a cake, that she had gotten rice and pineapple at the store. She told them she wished the current would flow both ways, like a tide, so that they could send her messages.

Now the treatment hit her like a dump truck. The previous exhaustion had been nothing compared to this final wave. She was more chilled than ever: wore her ski cap over her bald head continuously for warmth, and kept the fire roaring. She had already nearly depleted the second load of firewood and was beginning to look out the window at the forest, searching for the tree she would cut next. Her body felt as if her blood had been filled with lead. She was certain the doctors had made some mistake, had doubled or tripled her dose or had prescribed her a treatment for a three-hundred-pound football player; but she finished the treatment later that week and was free to return home to do nothing but shit and puke and sleep and cry.

She avoided her mirror — the blackened eyes, the astonishing weight loss, and the otherworldly fatigue — and settled in to wait. There were days when she did not get out of bed except to use the bathroom and empty her bedpan, and she felt certain she was dying, felt each day as if she had only one more day left. The doctors had gone too far, she was certain: had overcompensated for the challenge of the enemy.

She dreamed often that Shayna and Stephan came looking for her, that they could not find her and were disappointed. She dreamed that they were sending her notes in the river, or attempting to, but that the ships were all being carried away farther downstream, and ending up beached beside other people's cabins, or never found.

She dreamed that they came wandering through the woods, searching for her — that they found her cabin, but, unable to rouse her, left notes tacked to her door, and to the outside of the cabin walls — and then she dreamed that they no longer cared for her, were no longer interested in her.

She fell further into her dreams. The feeling that she was going to die soon left her. She began to imagine that she might survive for weeks, then months, and then even years.

They came over the mountain as they had said they would, with their arms and packs filled with sacks of food: loaves of bread, and servings of deer, elk, moose, and grouse, as well as a remnant of turkey carcass, and even some antelope, left over from a hunt their family had made to the eastern side of the state earlier in the fall.

They stepped up onto the porch, calling her name, arms too burdened with bounty to knock on the door, and when Jyl opened the door to greet them she saw that they were covered with snow, and they handed Jyl their bags one by one, and then knelt and unbuckled their snowshoes and slid off their heavy packs.

They had brought two jugs of apple cider, two gallons of

their own honey, jars of jam made from wild huckleberries, plums and strawberries they'd gathered from the valley; jars of smoked trout and whitefish, taken from the same creek on which she sailed her ships to them daily.

They had bags of dried mushrooms as well, morels and chanterelles, which represented but one of the hundreds of ways they made a living, and Jyl was touched not just by the dollar value of such gathered goods withdrawn from their hand-to-mouth seasonal income, but by the amount of labor that had gone into the gathering and then preparation of those foods.

The degree of their devotion to Jyl was evident on their faces — as if it were one of the great pleasures of their lives to be able to bring her these gifts.

The children stepped inside and put some food in the stove to warm — though the children had eaten a big mid-day meal with their family, they were famished again from their afternoon chores as well as the long hike over the mountain — and as the odors of warming food began to fill the cabin, the children sat at Jyl's feet on either side of her and helped her sketch the next ship, the design of which was the grandest yet, with their ambitions and imaginations having grown larger in the long absence of ships.

As Jyl drew, the children pointed to her sketch and suggested little additions and alterations: intricate carvings along the gunwales, a howling wolf on the bow. A keel made of a deer's rib, and the ivory from cow elk teeth and the incisors of deer decorating the deck like a mosaic of bright tile. Dollhouse furniture — a chest of drawers — fastened to the bow, so that the sketches and notes and stories could be stored in the tiny drawers. "Write a story with three chapters," Shayna urged her. "The first chapter can go in the top drawer, and the second chapter in the middle drawer, and the last chapter in the bottom drawer."

The food was warm again — they could detect its odors stirring — and they brought it to the table, and, after Stephan and Shayna said a prayer, the three of them ate with wordless focus, the children moving through their meal with startling intensity. They ate for an hour, attacking the meal in almost the precise manner with which they attacked any of their labors — working hard and methodically, yet deriving great pleasure from it, too — and when they were too full to eat any more (and yet, bounty still remained), they cleared their plates and dishes, and they and Jyl began carving that evening's ship, whittling it from one of the same lengths of pine that the children had cut for her firewood on their last visit.

Again the flakes of wood fell from her knife like petals of light or slivers of flame, and over the course of only about an hour the boat began to emerge, like a living thing working its way free of an egg or even a womb; and in the hour after that, they took turns sanding and polishing it. And though there were differences between the way they had sketched it on paper and the way it was turning out in real life, it was still a beautiful craft, and reflected well the care and attention they were giving it. And more than ever, as she watched the children work, Jyl had the thought that it was as if the children were hers — and not because she had made them hers with her love and attention, but vice versa: that they had claimed her. And she dreaded already the day when she would be released.

Soon enough — too soon, Jyl thought — the little boat was

ready to go, and, delighted, the children put it up on the mantel, proud of their work but excited, too, at the messages it would bring, over and over again.

The evening was still relatively young, and everyone was still relaxed from the big meal. The children were lying on the floor next to each other at right angles, their heads on pillows, absently fingering and twirling each other's hair rather than their own — as if despite the differences across the years they were somehow twins, or so like each other as to be the same, one self indistinguishable from the other.

Jyl took down from her windowsills several of the more alluring minerals she had found on her field trips, in the retracing and backtracking of her father's steps. Elbaite, also known as tourmaline; azurite, with malachite embedded. Hemimorphite, from Leadville, Colorado. A diamond, from Canada. Obsidian, from the Yellowstone country.

She let the children sort through them and handle them as she began another geology lecture. She told the children that there are only about four thousand known minerals on the planet: that of the finite elements trapped on the earth, there were only a finite number of arrangements or possibilities of composition available.

"Almost any mineral will form crystals," she told them. "A crystal is nothing more than an orderly, repeating atomic structure." She looked at Shayna and backed up for a moment, and told her about atoms — how they were the tiniest bricks in the world: that atoms in a rock were like atoms in a human being, or any other living creature.

She took her time lecturing, and watched the children examining the crystals before them. They did not want to set the minerals down but kept holding them, handling them.

"They start forming underground," she said, "when a few similar atoms cluster together, usually in water or lava, to form crystal seeds," she said. "As more and more atoms lock on to the seeds, they keep repeating that initial atomic arrangement so that the little seed crystal just keeps getting bigger and bigger, like a kind of blossoming."

Shayna raised her hand, and for the strangest moment Jyl had the feeling that she was going to ask her some question about God, or about her own beliefs, her chances of salvation. Instead Shayna asked, "Can an entire mountain be made of a crystal?" She was holding a piece of amethyst, peering through it at the lantern, and Jyl smiled, imagining what she was seeing, and said, "Absolutely. Most of those kinds of mountains are way underground. It's when they get exposed to the surface that they start getting broken apart and start crumbling, and being washed away." She nodded toward the amethyst. "The atomic structures of different minerals are what determine the mineral's shape, and its hardness — the way it responds to the world, and even the way it reacts to the world's light, giving each mineral its own unique color, its brilliance, its fire."

Stephan raised his free hand. In his other hand he held a lumpen, uncut ruby, as dark as a deer's heart.

"How long did it take to make this one?" he asked. Imagining some organic gestation involving perhaps months, or maybe even years.

Jyl smiled. "Probably a million years," she said.

She had thought they would be pleased by such a revelation, treasuring their crystals even more, and was surprised at first by the dismay that crossed their faces, until she understood or remembered that theirs was still a world in which miracles unfolded literally like the leaves on trees in the passing seasons, or as the blossoms of flowers emerged, or as ice melted, or snow fell, or as one simple match ignited one large fire.

She laughed, wanting to remind them that even a million years was not so long, but then remembered their fundamentalist upbringing and said nothing, and instead let them simply hold the rocks, let the weight of their mass, and their beautiful, inescapable density, speak the rocks' own truths to the children's hands.

They carved another ship later that night, a much smaller, simpler one requiring only about thirty minutes of work, and then, with Jyl fading quickly, suddenly — she lay down on the couch for a quick nap — the children went out into the snow to find yet another tree, to bring her more wood.

And again they felled and limbed it, then sawed and split it and hauled it to the porch, wearing a new path through the snow.

This time Jyl heard them thumping around on the porch — it was almost midnight — and she sat up and went out to praise them as they finished stacking enough wood for her to stay warm for another week.

They came inside to gather their bags and packs and empty dishes, and she loaded them down with several of the larger and more attractive gemstones, including a small diamond and an emerald. And though they protested at first, she could tell they were overjoyed with the gifts, and they promised to take good care of them forever; and it pleased her, watching them set off into the night, their one flashlight beam cutting a lane through the swirling flakes, to see that their packs were heavier, leaving, than they had been upon their arrival.

Another dream: the children's labors were hardening them, threatening to turn them to statues, even as Jyl's loneliness — the fiery, aching rawness of it — was keeping her alive. Consuming her, but in that burning giving life. The children were on a ship, they were leaving, being drawn away, years were passing in a single blink, a single thought, being pulled away by some current that hardened them and consumed her, until in the end none of them would remain as he or she had been, or even remain at all — only memory and stone, and yearning, like the wind.

She sat up with a shout, then got out of bed and accidentally kicked several of the rocks they had left on the floor, sent them skittering and clattering across the room.

With shaking hands she found her matches and lit a lantern, and began gathering the rocks. They were still holy to her, talismans, not only in that her father had discovered and claimed them, had deemed them worthy of preservation, but also because she determined now to give all of them to the children, whichever ones they desired; and after building a fire in her stove, using a little more of her precious supply of firewood, she began carving new ships. And because she was still chilled at first, her hands slipped once so that she cut her finger, causing the boat's bow to be smeared with her blood; and rather than sand it clean, she applied a symmetrical smear on the other side so that it seemed like a painted pattern.

When she was finished, she put a note, a story, and a crystal into the ship, walked down in the darkness to the even darker river, and turned the boat loose.

It was a yellow boat, and for a moment it looked like a spark, a live coal, in the river. Had her father ever dreamed or imagined, she wondered, that of the gems he brought back from the mountains any might ever undertake such paths and journeys? Such *motion*, and bringing such joy: almost as if they had had the breath of life breathed into them, and had become inspirited.

She continued to carve and send boats all during the next week, and then into December. Deer season had ended and a new silence fell upon the mountains, one that was welcome: Jyl did not mind that she had not gotten a deer. She had seen the giant king once, and that had been enough.

She continued to send messages, stories, and drawings, as well as gems and crystals and fossils — sending several out in the same day, staggered over different departure times — and in some of her drawings, as her loneliness grew, she would make little watercolor sketches of the three of them sitting around a table loaded with food, as they had at Thanksgiving, with gleaming candelabras casting a shining light upon a roast turkey, a wild goose, and all other manners of game upon their plates; and in the tiny rolled-up paintings there would be wreaths hanging on the walls, imges indicating the future, Christmas, rather than the past, Thanksgiving.

She never came right out and said, *I am lonely, please come back*, but as December moved forward and still her visitors, her friends, her little children, had not returned, she went even further with her pleadings and sketched a picture of her diminished woodpile.

She had been unable to get the saw to start once more, and though she still had a little wood left on her porch, she had taken to wandering the woods around her house, pulling down dead limbs and branches and ferrying them back to the house.

She was beginning to consider for the first time that the children might not be coming back.

They have grown up already, she feared. *They no longer care for me.*

The days grew ever shorter, plunging toward the solstice.

She tried not to panic. After all she had been through, this was still the worst.

She found herself standing at the window some days, watching for them, and staring at her woodpile — trying to conserve what she had, even though it made no sense, as this was the coldest time of year, and the children had not cut the wood for her to hoard, but rather to spend.

This newer, deeper, down-cutting loneliness was worse than the fears she had known before her diagnosis — those strange weeks when each traverse of the mountain had been more and more difficult — and worse than the first weeks after the diagnosis, the confirmation. This deeper loneliness was worse than the physical agony of the treatments, and worse than the captivity of the hospital room.

She moved around in her cabin, pacing, the walls lit with the wavering light cast by one of her lanterns as it sputtered out of propane. She was crying, pacing, crying, and when the one lantern finally blinked out she was too upset to connect it to a new bottle of propane but instead simply kept pacing, from darkness to light, darkness to light.

Soon the limitations of her physical frailty overtook her, so that she was exhausted and could pace no more. She collapsed onto her bed as if accepting her grave, and yet the loneliness continued — though finally she sank into a state of merciful catatonia, in which she stared unblinkingly at the ceiling until daylight, and then beyond.

The fire in her wood stove went out and still she did not move, but lay feeling the glaze of ice settle over her heart, feeling the salt residue of her tears dried to a taut mask across her face. And whereas most of her adult life she had felt as if she were always only a step or two or three behind her father, it seemed to her now that as she drew nearer to entering the place where he might be resting, he was paradoxically moving away from her again: an irony, now that she was so close.

She lay there, stunned, while the temperature in her cabin grew colder and colder and her fingertips grew numb and her face blue, and then she was shivering, her body having no fat to burn, no anything to burn, only spirit and bone; and then she was warm again, and her breathing was steadier, and, slowly, she felt the deep loneliness draining away, though still she was frightened.

She blinked and found herself focusing on one faint sound: as if she had traveled all that way, descending so far, to come into the presence of that one sound.

It was a tiny groaning sound, all around her: a sound of contraction, of pulling in. Every now and again it would make a single tick, as if living, or striving to live — sometimes two or three quick ticks in a row — before subsuming again into a slow, dull groan.

She listened to the sound, so near to her, for more than an hour before her chilled mind could make sense and clarity of it; and even then, the knowledge came to her like a kind of intuition, or memory.

It was the sound of her water pipes freezing. She was

aware of the great cold outside her cabin, the weight of it pressing down like a blanket, or like shovelfuls of loose dirt being tossed over the cabin — but in the final comfort of her numbness, she was surprised by the water's protest.

She lay there longer, listening and thinking. She could hear music; was this the sound her father heard now? Perhaps it was coming from her father's blood, the part of him which remained in her.

Surely he could hear what she was hearing now.

The pipes groaned louder and she blinked, then gasped, as another moment's clarity intruded: the duty and habit of living. She lay there for another half-hour, determining to get up and build a fire, if not to save the shred of her life, then to keep the pipes from freezing.

And in that time, she thought of nothing else but the goal of rising one more time. She lay there, trying to find the strength somewhere, like a pauper digging through empty pockets, searching again and again for the possibility of one more overlooked coin caught between the linty seams.

She imagined Stephan and Shayna finding her bedbound, blue, should they ever return, and the useless guilt they would shoulder, and she forced herself to find and feel a second surge of warmth.

Despite her numbed hands and legs, she slid out of bed, and with the smoothness of habit, the instruction of countless repetitions, she walked as if gliding, as if drawn, over to the cold stove, and crouched before it as if in prayer, then opened the door — a breath of cold air blew out, a breath like ice — and she crumpled some newspaper into it, and stacked a few toy sticks of kindling atop it — there was so little left now — and then lit a match.

The roar of the paper and kindling was deafening, and she

stared at the dancing fire, amazed at how something so silent a moment ago could make so much noise only an instant later.

Slowly she added more sticks to the fire and leaned in against the stove while it warmed, as one might rest against a sturdy horse; and when it grew too warm for comfort, she backed away and listened to the caterwauling of her pipes as the metal, and slushy ice within, creaked and groaned and stretched and contracted but did not break. Beginning again, and yet different this time.

She wouldn't do any more lost king stories in her boats to the children. She had found him. She had gone into his ice-bound room, and he had been sleeping. It had been dark in there, so she had never seen him, but she had been close, had heard him breathing.

He had sounded at peace. And she had left a part of herself in there with him. Or perhaps a part of her had always been with him, had remained with him forever: a part he had held all his life, and beyond, like a pebble, or a gem.

She waited until there was but a week left before Christmas, and then one more day — inside of a week — before determining that she had to humble herself and go over the mountain to find them, if they would not come to her. She could not imagine traveling so far, through such deep snow, even on snowshoes, but there was no choice — she had to see them. She worried that an ice jam might have breached the river, so that none of her ships were getting through, and lamented yet again that the family had no mailing address, and that once winter came, there was no way of getting in and out of their little valley save on foot or horseback, or by snowmobile.

It still astounded her to realize that as recently as a year ago she had been capable of running up and over the mountain, and then back, in a single day, a single afternoon.

She packed a lunch and sleeping bag, in case she had to stop and rest, and left before daylight, in a light falling snow. She had carved and painted presents for the children, little miniature toy rocking horses, but other than that, her pack was light.

The first hour was the hardest, as it contained the steepest ascent, and in the bulky snowshoes, she could travel only ten or twenty paces before having to stop and pant, not just to catch her breath but to still the quivering, the revolt of weakness, in her once-powerful legs, her thighs burning now as if aflame.

Gradually, however, she gained the elevation to the mountain pass and was able to walk along the level contour that led from her valley into theirs; and, thrilled by the knowledge that soon she would be seeing them, she took no notice of the time, and instead only leaned into the slanting snow, with the canyon below — carved long ago by the river's down-cutting — completely obscured by cloud and snow.

She knew the trail well, even in the almost sightless conditions — she knew it almost by touch, and by the pull of gravity — and she knew without even being able to see it when she had crossed the pass and come into their valley. She knew to descend, knew where the path was that led to the valley floor. It was the path of her life as well as of her dreams, and she could have gotten there blindfolded.

With her hair and eyebrows caked with snow and her face numb, Jyl reached the plowed and level field of their little garden — the autumn-turned furrows resting already beneath two feet of snow — and made her way into their yard, listening for any signs of activity, and then, as the shadowy shapes of the outbuildings and the cabin itself came into view, looking for a glow of light through the curtain of snow.

She was surprised by the absence of sound, and the absence of animals — the corral was open, and no barking dogs greeted her arrival, no chickens clucked or called from the henhouse. Their truck was gone, with no tracks in the snow to indicate it had been driven out recently, and when she came closer to the cabin, she saw with an emotion very close to panic and despair that no smoke was rising from the chimney.

They are asleep, she thought wildly, even though it was at least noon. *They worked so hard the day before that they are still asleep.*

When she drew even closer, she saw that the doors and windows were boarded up, and again, the drifts of snow against the door- and window-jambs indicated that they had been that way possibly for weeks: perhaps since the day after Thanksgiving.

She sat down on the steps in a daze, her mental and physical reserves equally devastated now.

Had they known they were leaving? she wondered: surely not. And yet she could not help but feel wounded: as if the children had somehow become frightened of her increasing need, her upwelling of loneliness, and had fled from that weight, that extra burden in their already burdened lives.

She knew it was not that way, that surely their itinerant parents had insisted they leave, for some unknown reason, perhaps economic, perhaps evangelical — leaving, summoned, in the midst of an evening meal, perhaps — but it was how she felt, that they had somehow become frightened of her.

Only the little boats remained, stacked up beneath one window. Out in the garden, gaunt deer pawed through the snow. The cabin was shut down yet preserved, protected, as if one day the travelers might return, though not for a long, long time — years, doubtless — and with the children by that time all grown up.

She sat down on the steps and began to cry. She cried for a long time, and when she had finished, she looked up — as if in her despair she might somehow have summoned them — and then wandered around and around the cabin, and out to the various barns and sheds. They had taken nearly every tool but had left an old short-handled shovel and a rusty hammer with one of its twin claws broken; and with these discards, she was able to pry away the boards over one of the windows and crawl into the cabin.

It was dark inside, with a strange still bluish light, as if she had entered a cave that had been closed off for centuries. They could not have been gone for more than two or three weeks, yet there was no residue whatsoever of their existence. The floor was swept and the walls were scrubbed, and all the furniture was gone, as was every other item — every spoon and fork, every dish and towel and article of clothing, every stick of firewood, every piece of kindling. Only a few more of the little ships remained, stacked neatly on the windowsills.

The gemstones that had been within the ships were gone, as were the drawings and stories. The boats sharpened her despair, for when, she asked herself, could she possibly ever use them again?

She ransacked the tiny drawers, all empty. *Write to me, think of me, speak to me,* she implored them, calling out to wherever they were.

Again and again, she searched through the cabin — examining every shelf, every cabinet, every drawer. She was a child. Had her father ever called out this way to her, after he had gone? If so, she had never heard him, and she feared the children could not hear her.

She crawled back out of the frigid, lonely cabin, and out into the great snowy silent whiteness of late December. She boarded the window back up tightly. She sat down on the steps and cried again, and it began to snow, as if her tears were somehow a catalyst for those flakes to form. As if the shapes and processes of all things followed from but an initial act, an initial law or pattern, like crystals repeating themselves. She sat very still, almost completely motionless, as the snow continued to cover everything, even the silent cabin. She concentrated on the tiny seed of fire housed in her chest. She sat very still, as if believing that, were she to move, even the slightest breeze would blow it out.

FIBER

I.

WHEN WE CAME into this country, runaways, renegades, we were like birds that had to sing. It was only ten years ago, but it feels like a hundred, or maybe a thousand. No person can know what a thousand years feels like, though in the first part of my life I was a geologist and was comfortable holding a footlong core of earth and examining such time — a thousand years per inch.

In the section of my life after that one, I was an artist, a writer of brief stories in which I was comfortable holding a sheaf of ten or twelve papers in which a lifetime, even several lifetimes, had passed. A few thousand people would read my slim books. They would write letters to me then and talk about the characters in those stories as if they were real people, which strangely saddened me.

Then came the third life. I became an activist. It was as if some wall or dam had burst within me, so that everything I wrote had to be asking for something — petition signatures, letters to Congress, and so on — instead of giving something.

But any landscape of significance — or power, whether dramatic or understated — will alter us if we will let it. And I am being bent yet again, though not without some fracturing; now I am into my fourth life, one built around things more immediate than the fairy-wing days of art. Even this narrative, this story, is fiction, but each story I tell feels like the last one I'll do — as if I've become like some insect or reptile trying to shed the husk of its old skin — and even now as I struggle toward the perceived freedom of the next phase of my life — the light ahead — neither you nor I can really be sure of how much of any story is fiction, or art, and how much of it is activism.

I am trying hard to move ahead cleanly into the next territory. But still, things slip and fall back; the old, even when it is buried beneath the new, sometimes rises and surges, pierces through, and reappears.

Sometimes it feels as if I am running toward the future, with a hunger for it, but other times as if I am simply fleeing the past, and those old skins. It's so hard not to look back.

I cut saw logs to sell to the mill. Prices are high, on the back of an election year (low interest rates, new housing starts), as the economies of man heat to incandescence, fueled by China's child labor, Mexico's slave labor — fueled by the five-dollar-per-hour slave labor even in our own country — and in sawing those logs the first thing I notice is whether the log I cut is an old tree or a young tree. I don't mean whether it's a big one or not; all the logs I cut are of roughly the same size — big enough so that I can almost get my arms around them. They are each a hundred inches long, a figure

I can measure off in my sleep, or can pace blindfolded. I've cut so many hundred-inch logs that I tend to see the world now in hundred-inch increments. That's the size log the L-P Mill over in Idaho needs for its laser mill, which makes short (eight-foot) two-by-fours. There's not a lot of waste. Those fucking lasers don't leave much kerf.

So the logs I cut are all about the same size, but each one is a different weight and density, depending mostly on age, and also on whether the tree got to be that big by growing quickly or slowly.

The first cut you make into the log will show you this — will tell you just about all you'd ever want to know about that tree's history. I can handle larger individual logs, and sometimes I'll hump some big-ass honker, tight green old-growth spruce or fir — four hundred fucking pounds packed into that hundred-inch length — but mostly I try to carry out only the medium-sized ones, which fill up the back of the truck quickly enough. Some of them will be eighty or ninety years old, if they grew slowly, in a shadowy light-starved place (the kind of woods where I best like to work in summer); and others, the same size, will be only twenty or thirty years old, with their growth rings spaced a quarter-inch apart or wider — trees that are seemingly composed of liquid sunlight, trees like pipe straws sucking up water and sucking down sunlight, trees of no real integrity or use, weakened from having grown too fast, and without ever having been tested.

But I get paid for volume, not quality, and I load them into the truck, too, a hundred inches at a time, though they feel as light as balsa wood after I've just handled an eighty- or ninety-year-old log before that one, and I feel guilty thinking of some carpenter three thousand miles away — Florida, perhaps — building some flimsy-shit house with those studs — the wood splitting like parchment at the first tap of a nail, and the carpenter cursing some unknowable thing, groping with his curse to reach all the way back to the point of origin, which is — what? The mill? Me? The sunlight? The brutality of supply and demand, and the omnipresent hyper-capitalism here at postconsumer century's end? Finish the house, stucco over the mistakes, paint it bright red and blue, sell the sonofabitch and move on. What're they going to do, dissect the house to cross-examine each strut, each stud? Who knows what's inside anything? More and more I'm trying not to look back at who I was, or even who I am, but at the land itself. I am trying to let the land tell me who and what I am — trying to let it pace and direct me, until it is as if I have become part of it.

This country — the Yaak Valley, way up in the northwest tip of Montana — burns and rots, both. The shape of the land beneath the forests is like the sluggish waves in an ancient, nearly petrified ocean — the waves of the northern Rockies sliding into the waves of the Pacific Northwest — so that it is like being lost, or like having found the rich, dense place you were always looking for. You can walk around any given corner and in less than a hundred paces go from fire-dependent ponderosa pine and grassland into the shadowy, dripping, mossy cedar-and-hemlock forests, rich with the almost sexual smell of rot. Tree frogs, electric red salamanders, hermit thrushes, ferns; climb a little farther, past the trickling waterfall, past the mossy green skull of a woodland caribou, and you come to a small glacier, across which are sculpted the transient, sun-melting tracks of where a wolverine passed the day before. The tracks and scourings of the glacier across the stone mountain, beneath all that ice, are only slightly less transient.

Down the sunny back side of the mountain, you can pass through one of the old 1910 burns, where there are still giant larch snags from that fire, each one a hollowed-out home to woodpeckers and martens and bear cubs. This old burned-out forest still has its own peculiar vital force and energy and seems almost to *seethe*, drunk or intoxicated on the health of so much available sunlight, and drunk on the health of the rich fire-blackened soil — the nutritiousness of ashes.

Then farther down the mountain, you'll be back into damp creekside silent old growth: more moss, and that dark Northwest forest — spruce and fir.

Back home, in your cabin, your dreams swirl, as if you are still traveling, still walking, even in your sleep, across this blessed landscape, with all its incredible diversity, and the strength that brings.

In the first life, back in Louisiana, I took things. Just the oil, at first, from so deep beneath the ground and from such a distant past that at first it did not seem like taking — but then, gradually and increasingly, from the surface.

I took boats, big boats, from their moorings at the marina at night: sailed them all night long — sometimes alone, other times with my wife, Hope. Before dawn we would sail back toward shore, then open the boat's drain plug to try to sink it, or sometimes we would even torch the boat, and swim back in that last distance to shore, and then watch, for a while, in the darkness, the beautiful flaming spectacle of unmitigated waste.

I would take everything, anything. The manhole covers to flood sewers in the street. License plates. Once, a sewing machine. From a backyard in suburban Lafayette, a picnic table. It was as if I were trying to eat the world, or that part of it. The newspapers began reporting the strange disappearances. They couldn't find any rhyme or reason to it — there seemed no logic in it.

I went in through windows and from dresser tops took jewelry and other riches. I didn't ever sell anything; I just took it. It pleased me. I would place the objects elsewhere. There are diamond necklaces hung in the boughs of cypress trees in Louisiana — pearl earrings in bird nests in the Atchafalaya.

I took cars: got in them and drove a short distance, then hid them, or sank them. It filled a need in me. I would look at my two hands and think, *What are these made for, if not to take?*

II.

I BELIEVE IN POWER. What I mean to say is, I ascribe great value to it, and like to observe power in action. I like the way continents are always straining to break apart or ride up on and over one another, and I like the way seedlings in the forest fight and scramble for light.

I like all that goes on in the hundred years of a tree's life, or the two hundred, or five hundred years of its span — all the ice and snow, the windstorms, the fires that creep around the edges of some forests and sweep through and across others, starting the process all over, and leaving behind a holy kind of pause, a momentary break in power before things begin to stretch and grow again, as vigorously as ever.

It feels good after sitting hunch-shouldered at a desk

these last ten or twelve years to be hauling real and physical things out of the woods: to get the green sweet gummy sap of fir stuck to my gloves and arms, to have the chunks of sawdust tumble from the cuffs of my overalls — to have the scent of the forest in my hair. The scent of leather gloves. The weight of the logs as real as my brief life, and the scent of blue saw smoke dense in my leather boots. The sight of bright new-cut yellow pinewood — a color that soon fades as it oxidizes, as the skin of a gleaming fish fades quickly, immediately after it dies, or as the hue of a river rock is lost forever after it is taken from the waters of its particular stream . . .

They can never find me here. They have been up here looking for me — with warrants — and may come again, but I have only to slip into the woods and disappear for a while. And perhaps this is where the activism came from, after the storytelling — the desire to defend a land that defended me. The desire to give, for once, after a lifetime of taking. Perhaps one reason none of us knows what's inside the heart or core of anything is that it's always changing: that things are always moving in a wave, or along an arc — and that the presence of one thing or one way of being indicates only that soon another will be summoned to replace it, as the night carves out the next day.

I thought I was made all along for writing short stories, and maybe one day again I will be, as forests recycle through succession, but this landscape has carved and fit me — it is not I who has been doing the carving — and I can feel, am aware of, my change, so that now what I best fit doing is hauling logs, one at a time.

I'm short — a low center of gravity — with short legs, but long arms, and a heart and lungs that don't get tired easily.

The red meat, the core of me, is stronger than ever. Certain accessories or trappings, such as ligaments, cartilage, disks, et cetera, are fraying and snapping — I get them mended, stitched back together, stapled and spliced or removed — but the rest of me is getting stronger, if slower, and I keep hauling the logs out one at a time, stepping gently over and around the fairy slippers and orchids, and choosing for my harvest only the wind-tossed or leaning trees, or the trees that are crowded too close together, or diseased. I try to select individual trees like notes of music. As one falls or is removed, others will rise, and with each cut I'm aware of this.

Art is selectivity — that which you choose to put in a story — and it's what you choose to leave out, too. This new life is still a kind of music, a kind of art, but it is so much more real and physical and immediate. It feels right to be doing this — hauling the logs out, carrying them over my shoulder one at a time like a railroad tie, some as dense and old as if soaked with creosote, or green life: and the more I carry, the stronger and more compact I get — the better I fit this job. As I choose and select, I listen to that silent music all around me, faint but real, of what I am doing: not imagining, but *doing*.

Sometimes I work in the rotting areas, other times in the burns. I become smeared with charcoal, blackened as if altered, and that night heading home I will stop and bathe in a stream and become pale again under the fierce stars, and will sometimes think about the days when I wrote stories, and then, further back, about the days when I practiced geology, and then, even further, to childhood and joy and wonder: but, without question, these days I am a black beast moving slowly through magical woods, growing shorter each year under these logs, as each year a disk is removed — as if I am sinking deeper and deeper into the old rot of the forest, until soon I'll be waist deep in the soil — and it is neither delicious nor frightening. It is only a fit.

A thing I do sometimes, when I have a log I'm really proud of, is to haul it out and carry it on my back and place it in the road next to some other logger's truck, or sometimes even in his truck, like a gift.

It is nothing more complex than trying to work myself out from under some imbalance of the past. I think that I will take a long time.

People are curious about who's doing it — the log fairy, they call him — and here, too, I take precautions not to get caught. I haul the heaviest, densest logs I can handle.

I know I'll get back to hauling the balsa-wood logs from the fields of light. I know it's not going to make a difference — but I try to select only the densest, heaviest blown-down logs from the old forests of darkness, and I try to envision them, after their passage to Idaho, or Texas, or wherever they go, as standing staunch and strong within their individual houses' frameworks. I picture houses and homes getting stronger, one at a time — one board at a time — as they feed on my magical forest, and then I imagine those strong homes raising strong families, and that they will act like cells or cores scattered across the country — like little stars or satellites — that will help shore up the awful sagging national erosions here at century's end. It's a fantasy, to be sure, but you tell me which is more real: an idea, such as a stated passion or desire of one human's emotions — susceptible to the vagaries of the world, and fading through time — or a hundred-inch, two-hundred-fifty-pound green juicy fir on one's mortal shoulder. You tell me which one is the fantasy and which is real.

I am so hungry for something real.

As I said, when we came up here to escape the law, we were artists: that second life. I breathed art — inhaled it, as the multinational timber companies are inhaling this forest's timber, and I exhaled it, too. It was easy to write stories, even poems. I don't even know what I'm doing, telling this one — only that for a moment, and one more time, it is as if I have stepped into a hole, or have put back on one of the old dry shed coats from an earlier time.

It was like a pulse, back then. There was an electricity between me and the land, and there was one between Hope and the land, too, and one between Hope and myself.

I'd work in my notebooks, sitting out at the picnic table, the sunlight bright on that paper, my pen curlicuing words and shapes across that parchment like lichens spreading across the page at time-lapse warp speed — and Hope would paint landscapes with oils, as she had done down in the South.

Back then she had worked in greens and yellows and had always walked around with dried smears of it on her hands and face, so that she seemed of the land, and of the seasons down there, as I tried to be — the incredibly fertile, almost eternal spring of greens and yellows, in Louisiana — but then, once we got up to this valley, the colors changed to blue fir, and blue rock, and to the white glaciers, and white clouds, and those became the colors affixed to her body, the residue of her work. There are four distinct seasons up here, as in some child's fairy-tale book, except that after Louisiana's slow motion, the seasons in Yaak seem almost to gallop — the quick burning flash of dry brown heat, *August*, then an explosion of yellow and red, *October*, then more blue and white, blue and white, then winter's black-and-whiteness, seeming to last forever but snatched away finally by the incandescence of true spring — even now, after a decade (the trees in the forest around us another inch larger in diameter, since that time). Hope is still searching to settle into the rhythms of this place — the fast rhythms of the surface, as well as the slower ones frozen in the rock below.

Between her chores of running the household and helping raise the children, I do not see much blue paint smeared on her, or any other color. And we just don't talk about art anymore. An overwhelming majority of the art that we see discourages us, depresses us — no longer inspires us — and whether this is a failure within us or one with the artists of this age, we're not sure.

It seems like a hundred years ago, not ten, since we first came up here. Back then I would stumble through the forest, pretending to hunt — sometimes taking a deer or an elk or a grouse — but mostly I would just think about stories: about what had to be at stake in any given story, and about the orthodox but time-tested critical progressions, or cyclings, of beginning-middle-end, and of resolutions within a story, and epiphanies — all the old things. They were new to me back then, and seemed as fresh as if none of it had ever been done before.

I did not know the names of the things past which I was walking, or the cycles of the forest, or the comings and goings, lives and deaths, the migrations of the animals. At night, hiking home after I'd traveled too far or been gone too long, I did not know the names of things by their scent alone as I passed them in the darkness.

Those kinds of things came to me, though, and are still coming, slowly, season after season, and year after year; and it is as if I am sinking deeper in the earth, ankle-deep in mulch now. I keep trying to move laterally — am drawn laterally — but recently it has begun to feel as if perhaps the beginnings of some of my old desires are returning — my diving or burrowing tendencies: the pattern of my entering the ground vertically again, as I did when I was drilling for oil, desiring to dive again, as if believing that for every emotion, every object, every landscape on the surface, there is a hidden or corresponding one at depth. We tend to think there are clean breaks between sections of anything, but it is so rarely that way, in either nature or our own lives: things are always tied together, as the future is linked, like an anchor, to the past.

Hope and I don't talk about art anymore. We talk about getting our firewood in for winter, or about the deer we saw that day. We talk about the wildflowers, or the colors of the leaves — that's the closest we come to discussing the shadow or memory of her work — and we do not come close to discussing mine, either, or the memory or buried shadow of it. We talk about *things*, instead, and hand things to each other, for us to touch: a stone found on the mountain that day, or an irregular piece of driftwood. A butterfly, wind-plastered and dried, pinned to the grille of the truck, looking remarkably like the silk scarves and blouses she used to paint. We step carefully, desiring to travel further into this fourth life, being pulled into it by unknown or rather unseen rhythms.

Walking quietly, carefully, as if believing that perhaps we can sneak away from those old lives and be completely free of them, and in pace — once more — with the land.

The logs that get you are almost always late in the day. You overextend, in your love, your passion for the work, the delicious physicality of it — the freedom of being able to work without acknowledging either a past or a future.

You spy a perfect fallen tree just a little bit out of your reach, at the bottom of a steep slope. You have to cross a tangle of blowdown to get to it. It's a little larger than you should be carrying and a little too far from the truck — you've already hauled a day's worth — but all of these things conspire within you, as you stare at the log, to create a strange transformation or alteration: they reassemble into the reasons, the precise reasons, that you *should* go get that log.

And, always, you do, so that you will not have to go to bed that night thinking about that log and how you turned away from it.

III.

THERE ARE seventy-six species of rare and endangered plants in this forest — Mingan Island moonwort, kidney-leaved violet, fringed onion, maidenhair spleenwort — and I know them all, each in both its flowering and dormant states. Most of them prefer the damp dark depths of the last corners of old growth up here, though others prefer the ashes of a new fire and appear only every two hundred years or so.

Still others seek the highest, windiest, most precarious existences possible, curled up in tiny clefts at the spartan tops of mountains, seeking brief moisture from the slow, sun-glistening trickle of glaciers. I know all of them, and I watch carefully as I walk with the log across my back, across both shoulders like a yoke. Again it is like a kind of slow and deliberate, plodding music — the music of humans — choosing and selecting which step to place so as to avoid those seventy-six species, whenever I am fortunate enough to find any of them in the woods where I am working. They say the list is growing by a dozen or so each year. They say before it's all over there won't be anything but fire ants and dandelions. They say . . .

That is my old life. This is my new one. My newest one. This one feels different — more permanent.

Still, the old one, or old ones, try to return. My right side's stronger than my left, so I use it more. By the end of the day it's more fatigued than the left, and it feels sometimes as if I'm being turned into a corkscrew; and because of this slight imbalance, accumulated and manifested over time, my steps take on a torque that threatens to screw me down deeper and deeper into the ground, like the diamond drill bits I'd fasten to the end of the pipe string when I worked in the oil fields. And late in the day I find myself once again day-dreaming about those buried landscapes, and other hidden and invisible things.

A midnight run to town with four gleaming, sweet-smelling larch logs — hundred-inch lengths, of course, and each one weighing several hundred pounds. A cold night: occasional star showers, pulsing of northern lights, sky electricity. Coyote yappings on the outskirts of town. A tarp thrown over the back of my truck, to hide the logs. One in one logger's truck, another in his neighbor's truck. So silent. They will think it is a strange dream when they look out in the morning and see the gift trees, the massive logs, but when they go out to touch them they will be unable to deny the reality.

The third log into the back of yet another sleeping logger's truck, and the fourth one in the front yard of the mill itself, standing on end, as if it grew there overnight.

Home, then, to my wife and children and the pursuit of peace, and balance. In the winter, Hope and I sleep beneath the skins, the hides, of deer and elk from this valley.

There is an older lady in town who works on plow horses — gives them rubdowns, massages, hoists their hips and shoulders back into place when they pop out — she says they're easy to work with, that a horse won't tense up and resist you when you press or lean against its muscles — and when my back gets way out of line, I go visit her and she works on it. I lie on her table by the wood stove while she grinds her elbow and knee into certain pressure points, and she pulls and twists, trying to smooth it all back into place, and she uses a machine she calls "Sparky," too, which I have never seen, as she uses it only on my back. It sends jolts of electricity deep into my muscles — which, she says, are but electrical fibers, like cables, conduits for electricity — and the sound that Sparky makes as she fires round after round of electricity into me (my legs and arms twitching like some laboratory frog's) is like that of a staple gun.

And sometimes I imagine that it is: that she is piecing me back together, that she is pausing, choosing and selecting which treatments to use on me that day, so that I can go back out into the woods to choose and select which wood to take out and send to the far-away mills, who will then send the logs to . . .

We are all still connected, up here. Some of the connections are in threads and tatters, tenuous, but there is still a net of connectivity through which magic passes.

Whenever a new car or truck enters the valley, I run and hide. I scramble to the top of a hill and watch through the trees as it passes. They can never get me. They would have to get the land itself.

The scent of sweat, of fern, of hot saw blade, boot leather, damp bark; I suck these things in like some starving creature. All the books in my house now sit motionless and unexamined on their shelves, like the photos of dead relatives, dearly loved and deeply missed. Sometimes I pull them down, touch the spines, even say their names aloud, as one would the name of one's mother, "Mom," or one's grandmother, "Grandma."

But then I go back out into the woods.

Once, carrying a log across a frozen pond, I punched through the ice and fell in up to my chest — the cold water such a shock to my lungs that I could barely breathe — and I had to drop the log and skitter out, then build a quick fire to warm up. (The heater in my old truck doesn't work.) Some days, many days, it feels like two steps forward and two steps back, as the land continues to carve and scribe us at its own pace, not ours.

And now when I take my pickup truck to the mill and off-load my logs next to the millions of board feet that are streaming through it like diarrhea through a bloated pig's butt in the feedlot — what difference do I think it will make? How does my fantasy stand up then, under the broad examination of reality?

In protest, I haul the logs more slowly than ever. In protest, I take more time with them. I touch them, smell them.

I tithe the best ones to strangers. Sometimes I sit down and read the cross section of each log, counting the growth rings. Here is where one seedling grew fast, seeking light, struggling for co-dominance. Here is where it reached the canopy and was then able to put more of its energy into girth and width rather than height — *stability*. Here — this growth ring — is the drought year; then the succession of warm, wet growing years. Here — the next band of rings — is where the low-intensity fire crept through around the forest, scorching the edges of but not consuming the tree.

I read each of the logs in this manner, as if reading the pages of some book. Maybe someday I will go back to books. Maybe someday I will be drawn to submerge back into the vanished or invisible world and will live and breathe theory, and maybe Hope will start painting again.

But right now I am hauling logs, and she is gardening, raking the loose earth with tools, though other times with her bare hands, and it feels as though we are falling, and as if we are starving, and as if I must keep protesting, must keep hauling logs.

We try not to buy anything, anymore — especially nothing made of wood. It's all such utter, flimsy shit. One touch, one stress upon it, and it all splinters to hell — a hammer or ax handle, a wooden stepladder, a chest of drawers . . . It is all such hollow shit, and we are starving.

Before I burned out in that third life, I was asizzle. I remember awakening each morning to some burning smell within me — scorched metal against metal. Manatees, ivory-billed woodpeckers, whales, wolves, bears, bison — I burned for it all, and did so gladly. The forest loves its fires.

The reason I think I left the second life — left art, left storytelling — was because it had become so safe, so submerged. It wasn't radical enough. They say most people start out being radical when they are young and then gravitate toward moderation in middle age, and then beyond moderation, to the excesses of the right — but for me it has been the opposite — as if the land itself up here is inverted, mysterious, even magical — turning humans, and all else, inside out, in constant turmoil, constant revolution.

We — all painters and writers — don't want to be political. We want to be pure, and *artistic*. But we all know, too, I think, that we're not up to the task. What story, what painting, does one offer up to refute Bosnia, Somalia, the Holocaust, Chechnya, China, Afghanistan, or Washington, D.C.? What story or painting does one offer up to counterbalance the ever-increasing sum of our destructions? How does one keep up with the pace? Not even the best among us is up to this task, though each tries; like weak and mortal wood under stress, we splinter, and try to act, create, heal. Some of us fall out and write letters to Congress, not novels; others of us write songs, but they are frayed by stress and the imbalance of the fight. Some of us raise children, others raise gardens. Some of us hide deep in the woods and learn the names of the vanishing things, in silent, stubborn protest.

I want to shock and offend. Hauling *logs?* My moderation seems obscene in the face of what is going on on this landscape, and in this country — the things, the misery, for which this country is so much the source rather than a source of healing or compassion.

Paint me a picture or tell me a story as beautiful as other things in the world today are terrible. If such stories and paintings are out there, I'm not seeing them.

I do not fault our artists for failing to keep up with, or hold in check, the world's terrors. These terrors are only a phase, like a fire sweeping across the land. Rampant beauty will return.

In the meantime, activists blink on and off like fireflies made drowsy over pesticide-sodden meadows. Activism is becoming the shell, the husk, where art once was. You may see one of them chained to a gate, protesting yet another Senate-spawned clear-out, and think the activist is against something, but the activist is for something, as artists used to be. The activist is for a real and physical thing as the artist was once for the metaphorical; the activist, or brittle husk-of-artist, is for life, for sensations, for senses deeply touched: not in the imagination, but in reality.

The activist is the emergency room doctor trying to perform critical surgery on the artist. The activist is the artist's ashes.

And what awaits the activist's ashes: peace?

IV.

THERE IS, of course, no story: no broken law back in Louisiana — no warrant, no fairy logs. I am no fugitive, other than from myself. Here, the story falls away.

It — storytelling — has gotten so damn weak and safe. I say this not to attack from within, only to call a spade a spade: a leftover lesson from art. I read such shit, and see such shit paintings, that I want to gag; one could spray one's vomit across the canvas and more deeply affect or touch the senses — what remains of them — than the things that are spewing out into the culture now.

The left has vanished, has been consumed by the right. On one day the Sierra Club announces it is against all logging in national forests — "zero cut" — and the next day it turns around and endorses for reelection President Clinton, who has just endorsed the industrial liquidation of five billion board feet of timber in one year alone. Hell yes, employment is up this year, but what about after the reelection, when the five billion drops back to zero, because it's all been cut or washed by erosion? Clinton tosses in the Tongass National Forest in Alaska — old growth coastal rain forest — gives the timber company a one-hundred-year lease on it. And the Sierra Club, bastion of radicalism, endorses him.

Trying to shore up his base among the environmentalists — a long nasty word for which we should start substituting "human fucking beings" — Clinton designates a couple million acres of Utah desert as a national monument; the year before, he signed a Senate bill protecting California desert. He's made some moves in the direction of protecting some Pacific Northwest old growth, too, but nothing for the Yaak; whether planned or not, he is making a political trade of rock for timber — trading the currency of Yaak's wildness for votes and red rock — and this is an alteration, a transformation, which will not bear scrutiny: it is not grounded in reality, it cannot be done, it is surficial, flimsy, it is theft. He is not the environmental president. He is trading rock for timber. Each has its inherent values, but each is different.

The Yaak, perched up on the Canadian line like some hunch-shouldered griffin high in a snag, looking down on the rest of the American West, can act as a genetic pipeline to funnel its wild creatures and their strange, magical blood down into Yellowstone and the Bitterroot country, and back out toward the prairies, too. It can still resurrect wildness. There is still a different thrumming in the blood of the Yaak's inhabitants.

The damn Nature Conservancy won't even get involved up here. The timber companies owned the land along the river bottoms in the Yaak, and they clear-cut those lands and left town rather than waiting for the trees to grow back as they're always bragging they'll do. But before leaving town (shutting down the mill behind them, so that now we have to export our wood, and jobs, to Idaho), the big timber companies subdivided the hell out of those clear-cut lands, turned them into ranchettes like cow turds all up and down the river, and still I couldn't get the damn Conservancy to become active up here.

When I wrote to them, they wrote back and told me the valley wasn't important enough. They hadn't ever seen the damn place. Now the vice president of the timber company — Plum Creek — that's selling off these lands in such tiny fragments sits on the board of directors of the Nature Conservancy.

I don't mean to speak ill of anyone, and certainly not of a man I've never met, but Plum Creek's got several tens of thousands of acres in the south end of the Yaak, in the Fisher River country, which is the only route by which a wandering grizzly can pass down out of the Yaak and into the rest of the West.

Plum Creek owns the plug, the cork, to the bottleneck — these lands were given to them by Congress more than a hundred years ago — and so now the situation is that one man — one human, more heroic than any artist or group of artists ever dreamed of being — will do either the right thing and protect that land, or the wrong thing and strangle the last wildness.

If you think I'm going to say please after what they've already done to this landscape, you can think again. It is not about being nice or courteous. It is not even about being radical. It is simply about right versus wrong, and about history: that which has already passed, and that which is now being written and recorded.

I can hear my echo. I recognize the tinny sound of my voice. I know when an edge is crossed, in art: when a story floats or drifts backward or forward, beyond its natural confines. And I understand that I am a snarling wolverine, snapping illogically at everything in my pain, snapping at everyone — at fellow artists, and at fellow environmentalists.

I am going to ask for help, after all. I have to ask for help. This valley gives and gives and gives. It has been giving more timber to the country for the last fifty years than any other valley in the Lower Forty-eight; and still not one acre of it is protected as wilderness.

I load the logs slowly into the back of my ragged truck and drive them to the mill in protest. The valley cannot ask for anything — can only give — and so like a shell or husk of the valley I am doing the asking, and I am the one saying please, at the same time that I am also saying, in my human way, fuck you.

Somebody help. Please help the Yaak. Put this story in the president's or vice president's hands. Or read it aloud to one of them by firelight on a snowy evening with a cup of cider within reach, resting on an old wooden table.

The firelight on the spines of books on the shelf, flickering as if across the bones or skeletons of things; and outside, on that snowy night, the valley holding tight to the eloquence of a silence I can no longer hear over the roar of my own saw.

Somebody please do this. Somebody please help.

— Yack, Montana, 1998

THE WINDY DAY

THE LAST DAY of my life before I knew what I would be the father of — a son or a daughter — was a good one. It was in October, the fourth month, and there'd been high winds flapping the tin on our cabin roof all through the night. We woke up thinking, *This is the day we drive to town and find out.*

That morning there was smoke all through the valley, an eerie green fog, and the taste of smoke was everywhere, and ash was falling from the sky like snow.

We sat around in that strange green light that we had never seen before and waited until it was time to leave for town. The wind was gusting to sixty and then seventy miles an hour. We could hear trees crashing in the forest. I knew there'd be some trees down across the road, but I had no idea how many.

"Maybe we should wait," Elizabeth said.

I think she meant wait another month, or even the remaining five months.

But I was ready. I had waited thirty-three years already. Waiting's fine up to a point. I was ready. I was pretty sure I was ready.

The tops of trees were blowing through the sky. The forest was being rent apart, tunnels of wind snapping their way through the great forever larch trees, breaking them off up high, where the winds were gustier: seventy, eighty, ninety miles an hour.

Ash was rushing everywhere.

I loaded the chain saw, extra gas and oil, and wrenches into the back of the truck; loaded up an overshirt and my heavy leather gloves. It would be okay to show up at the hospital with just a little bit of gasoline and wood chips on me. It was Elizabeth who was going to get tested — ultrasounded — not me. I was just going to stand there and hold her hand, and watch the screen.

Deer and moose were running through the woods, not knowing, as we did, that the fire was still fifteen miles away, that it was still safe, just smoky.

And windy.

I had to stop and cut a tree about every hundred yards or so in the first mile. But that was okay. It was exciting — all those branches and boughs floating past, some of them caught in dust-devil swirls high over our heads. It was midday, but growing so dark from the ash and smoke that we had our headlights on — almost as dark as night, but in that strange *green* way. Sometimes the vague light would grow so suddenly dim that it was as if someone were dimming it on purpose, the glow fading almost away and the blackness coming on, night in the middle of the day. But then it would turn green again, the dullest light, and I would make two neat cuts in each tree and roll the log off to the side of the road and pass through, on to the next tree.

"We have to be careful," Elizabeth shouted as the trees fell all around us.

"Do you want to go back?" I asked once.

"No," she said.

We watched ahead of us, and to the side, to be careful not to be pinned by any falling trees. The wind was so strong and indecisive that you couldn't tell which way the trees were going to fall until they snapped. Sometimes we'd see them fall in the woods; other times we'd see them fall across the road just in front of us and farther on up the road. The trees were falling behind us, too, closing off our return, but that didn't matter.

It was twelve miles out to the main road, and after that I hoped it would get better. The road was a little wider out there, and maybe someone with a chain saw would have already gone through ahead of us.

I moved slowly but steadily. There wasn't any rush. I liked cutting the fallen trees and moving them to one side. Carrying my wife and child — *child* — through the storm. I didn't think of the trees as being dangerous or my enemy. I had to be careful and look up when I was cutting because I couldn't hear the snap and crack and splinter when the saw was running. Elizabeth, in the truck, had to look up and all around and make sure nothing fell on top of the truck while she was in it. I tried to park it next to ridges or high banks so that a falling tree would land against the road bank rather than crashing all the way down onto the truck.

I had not wanted to know, and had not wanted to know,

but then I suddenly wanted to know. It was just a windy day. Maybe a little too windy. But it is so hard to turn back. Some of the trees were so big. Gold-needled larch boughs carpeted the narrow road, branches upturned like torn arms. The woods smelled heavily of smoke but also of fresh sap. It was a crisp, heady smell that made me want to keep cutting all the way to Libby, more than forty miles away. Which was where we were going. We hadn't yet realized there would be even more trees down across the main road.

We got to the main road about an hour before dark. We'd long since missed our appointment. But I didn't care, I was revved up, had long ago fallen into the mood of the crashing forest — cut cut roll, drive on, cut cut roll, drive on. Treetops were still hurtling past us as if in a hurricane, and that dense green smoky light was pulsing and darkening, dimming and glimmering, and giving way to true dark.

"Let's go back," Elizabeth said finally. We still had nearly forty miles to go. "We can try again tomorrow," she said.

I didn't want to go back. It seemed an impossibility for me to go back. We had cut our way out to the main road. I still had the saw in my hands and plenty of gas left. It was dark. But I still had that saw in my hands.

"Okay," I said.

Though if it was a girl, in sixteen years the two of us would be riding horses through these very woods, leaping some of the rotting logs that had fallen this day, riding through sweet fir-scented woods in the autumn on fine muscular horses whose bellies creaked and who farted wildly with each jump, each lift and gather over the fallen logs; and if it was a boy, in sixteen years we would be pulling logs out of the woods, fastening cables to them and pulling them through the woods with those very same horses, in that same autumn, to repair the buck-and-rail fence that another wind had disrupted.

I still had the saw in my hands.

"Okay," I said, branches and limbs floating and drifting through the thick ashy air like streamers and kites, pieces of trees rising and falling on all the hot, smoky, crazy currents, trees swaying from side to side, popping and snapping, and Elizabeth and me guarding what we had, what we were taking with us, out of the woods and into the future, watching all around us for those devil falling snags, those crashing trees; and me with the saw, inching our way through the wreckage, the fresh sweet smell of sap and crushed boughs, cutting our thin lane straight through the forest to the light.

G O A T S

I T   W O U L D   B E   E A S Y to say that he lured me into the fields of disrepair like Pan, calling out with his flute to come join in on the secret chaos of the world: but I already had my own disrepair within, and my own hungers, and I needed no flute call, no urging. I've read recently that scientists have measured the brains of adolescent boys and have determined that there is a period of transformation in which the ridges of the brain swell and then flatten out, becoming smoother, like mere rolling hills, rather than the deep ravines and canyons of the highly intelligent, and that during this physiological metamorphosis it is for the boys as if they have received some debilitating injury, some blow to the head, so that, neurologically speaking, they glide, or perhaps stumble, through the world as if in a borderline coma during that time.

Simple commands, much less reason and rules of consequence, are beyond their ken, and if heard at all sound perhaps like the clinking of oars or paddles against the side of a boat heard by one underwater, or like hard rain drumming on a tin roof, as if the boys are wearing a helmet of iron against which the world, for a while, cannot, and will not, intrude.

In this regard, Moxley and I were no different. We heard no flute calls. Indeed, we heard nothing. But we could sense the world's seams of weaknesses — or believed we could — and we moved toward them.

Moxley wanted to be a cattle baron. It wasn't about the money — we both knew we'd go on to college, Moxley to Texas A&M and me to the University of Texas, and that we'd float along in something or another. He wanted to become a veterinarian, too, in addition to a cattle baron — back then, excess did not seem incompatible with the future — and I thought I might like to study geography. But that was all eons away, and in the meantime the simple math of cattle ranching — one mother cow yielding a baby, which yielded a baby, which yielded a baby — appealed to us. All we had to do was let them eat grass. We had no expenses: we were living at home, and we just needed to find some cheap calves. The money would begin pouring in from the cattle, like coins and bills from their mouths. With each sale we planned to buy still more calves — four more from the sale of the fatted first one, then sixteen from the sale of those four, and so on.

I lived in the suburbs of Houston with both my parents (my father was a geologist, my mother a schoolteacher), neither of whom had a clue about my secret life with cattle (nor was there any trace of ranching in our family's history), while Moxley lived with his grandfather, Old Ben, on forty acres of grassland about ten miles north of what were then the Houston city limits.

Old Ben's pasture was rolling hill country, gently swelling, punctuated by brush and thorns — land that possessed only a single stock tank, a single aging tractor, and a sagging, rusting barbed-wire fence good for retaining nothing, with rotting fence posts.

Weeds grew chest high in the abandoned fields. Old Ben had fought in the first World War as a horse soldier and had been injured repeatedly, and was often in and out of the V.A. clinic, having various pieces of shrapnel removed, which he kept in a bloodstained gruesome collection, first on the windowsills of their little house but then, as the collection grew, on the back porch, scattered in clutter, like the collections of interesting rocks that sometimes accrue in people's yards over the course of a lifetime.

Old Ben had lost most of his hearing in the war, and some of his nerves as well, so that even on the days when he was home, he was not always fully present, and Moxley was free to navigate the rapids of adolescence largely unregulated.

We began to haunt the auction barns on Wednesdays and Thursdays, even before we had our driver's licenses — skipping school and walking there, or riding our bikes — and we began to scrimp and save, to buy at those auctions the cheapest cattle available: young calves, newly weaned, little multicolored lightweights of uncertain pedigree, costing seventy or eighty dollars each.

We watched the sleek velvety gray Brahma calves, so clearly superior, pass on to other bidders for $125, or $150, and longed for such an animal; but why spend that money on one animal when for the same amount we could get two?

After parting with our money we would go claim our

prize. Sometimes another rancher offered to put our calf in the back of his truck or trailer and ferry it home for us, though other times we hobbled the calf with ropes and chains and led it, wild and bucking, down the side of the highway, with the deadweight of a log or creosote-soaked railroad tie attached behind it like an anchor to keep the animal — far stronger, already, than the two of us combined — from breaking loose and galloping away unowned and now unclaimed, disappearing into the countryside, our investment now no more than a kite snatched by the wind.

We gripped the calf's leash tightly and dug in our heels, and were half hauled home by the calf itself. In the creature's terror it would be spraying and jetting algae-green plumes of excrement in all directions, which we would have to dodge, and were anyone to seek to follow us — to counsel us, perhaps, to turn away from our chosen path, still experimental at this point — the follower would have been able to track us easily, by the scuffed-up heel marks and divots of where we had resisted the animal's pull, and by the violent fans of green-drying-to-brown diarrhea: the latter an inauspicious sign for an animal whose existence was predicated on how much weight it would be able to gain, and quite often the reason these marginal calves had been sent to the auction in the first place.

Arriving finally at Moxley's grandfather's farm, bruised and scratched, and with the calf in worse condition, we would turn it loose into the wilderness of weeds and brambles circumscribed by the sagging fence.

We had attempted, in typical adolescent half-assed fashion, to shore up the fence with loose coils of scrap wire, lacking expertise with the fence stretcher, and in some places where we had run out of wire we had used the orange nylon twine gathered from bales of hay, and lengths of odd-sorted rope, to weave a kind of cat's cradle, a spider web of thin restraint, should the calf decide to try and leave our woolly, brushy, brittle pasture.

We had woven the fence with vertical stays also, limbs and branches sawed or snapped to a height of about four feet, in the hopes that these might help to provide a visual deterrent, so that the curving, staggering, collapsing fence looked more like the boundaries of some cunning trap or funnel hastily constructed by Paleolithics in an attempt to veer some driven game toward slaughter.

We had money only for cattle or fence, but not both. Impulsive, eager, and impatient, we chose cattle, and the cattle slipped through our ramshackle fence like the wind itself — sometimes belly-wriggling beneath it, other times vaulting it like kangaroos.

Other times the calves simply went straight through the weakened fence, popping loose the rusted fence staples and shattering the rotted, leaning fence posts and crude branches stacked and piled as barricades. Sometimes the calves, fresh from the terror and trauma of their drive from auction, never slowed when first released through the gate at Old Ben's farm, but kept running, galloping with their heads lowered all the way down the hill, building more and more speed, and they would hit the fence square on.

Sometimes they would sail right on through it, like a football player charging through the paper stretched between goalposts before a football game, though other times they would bounce back in an awkward cartwheel before scrambling to their feet and running laterally some distance until they found a weaker seam and slipped through it not like anything of this world of flesh and bone, but like magicians, vanishing.

When that happened, we would have to leap on the old red tractor, starting it with a belch and clatter that inevitably frightened the calf into even wilder flight; and with Moxley driving the old tractor flat-out in high gear, and me standing upright with a boot planted wobbily on each of the sweeping wide rear fenders, riding the tractor like a surfer and swinging a lariat (about which I knew nothing), we would go racing down the hill after the calf, out onto the highway, the tractor roaring and the calf running as if from some demon of hell that had been designed solely to pursue that one calf, and which would never relent.

We never caught the calves, and only on the rarest of occasions were we ever even able to draw near enough to one — wearing it down with our relentlessness — to even attempt a throw of the lariat, which was never successful.

Usually the animal would feint and weave at the last instant, as the tractor and whizzing gold lariat bore down on it, and would shoot or crash through another fence, or cross a ditch and vault a fence strung so tightly that as the calf's rear hoofs clipped the fence going over, the vibration would emit a high taut hum, which we could hear even over the sound of the tractor.

It was like the sound of a fishing line snapping, and by the time we found an unlocked gate to that pasture the calf would have escaped to yet another field, or might be down in some creek bottom, reverting to instincts more feral and cunning than those of even the deer and turkeys that frequented those creeks; and we would scour the surrounding hills for all the rest of that day — sometimes mistakenly pursuing, for a short distance, a calf that might look like ours, until that calf's owner would come charging out on his own tractor, shouting and cursing, angling to intercept us like a jouster.

Old Ben fell too ill to drive and then began to become a problem while Moxley was in school; he had begun to wander out into the same fields in which the rogue calves had been released, and was similarly trying to escape his lifelong home, though he was too feeble to bash or batter his way through the patchwork fence and instead endeavored to climb over it.

Even on the instances when he made good his escape, he snagged his shirt or pants on a barb and left behind flag-size scraps of bright fabric fluttering in the breeze, and we were able to track him that way, driving the roads in his old station wagon, searching for him.

Sometimes Old Ben lay down in a ditch, trembling and exhausted from his travels, and pulled a piece of cardboard over him like a tent to shield him from the heat, and we would pass on by him, so that it might be a day or two before we or a neighbor could find him.

Other times, however, Old Ben would become so entangled in his own fence that he would be unable to pull free, and when we came home from school we would see him down there, sometimes waving and struggling though other times motionless, quickly spent, with his arms and legs akimbo, and his torn jacket and jeans looking like the husk from some chrysalis or other emerging insect; and we'd go pluck him from those wires, and Moxley mended his torn jacket with the crude loops of his own self-taught sewing: but again and again Old Ben sought to flow through those fences.

There were other times though when Old Ben was fine, fit as a fiddle; times when the disintegrating fabric of his old war-torn mind, frayed by mustard gas and by the general juices of war's horror, shifted like tiny tectonic movements, reassembling into the puzzle-piece grace his mind had possessed earlier in life — the grandfather Moxley had known and loved, and who loved him, and who had raised him. On those occasions it felt as if we had taken a step back in time. It was confusing to feel this, for it was pleasant; and yet, being young, we were eager to press on. We knew we should be enjoying the time with Old Ben — that he was not long for the world, and that our time with him, particularly Moxley's, was precious and rare, more valuable than any gold, or certainly any rogue cattle.

On the nights when the past reassembled itself in Old Ben and he was healthy again, even if only for a while, the three of us ate dinner together. We sat on the back porch feeling the Gulf breezes coming from more than a hundred miles to the southeast, watching the tall ungrazed grass before us bend in oceanic waves, with strange little gusts and accelerations stirring the grass in streaks and ribbons, looking briefly like the braids of a rushing river, or as if animals in hiding were running along those paths, just beneath the surface and unseen.

We would grill steaks on the barbecue, roast golden ears of corn, and drink fresh-squeezed lemonade, to which Ben was addicted. "Are these steaks from your cattle?" he would ask us, cutting into his meat and examining each bite as if there might be some indication of ownership within; and when we lied and told him yes, he seemed pleased, as if we had amounted to something in the world, and as if we were no longer children. He would savor each bite, then, as if he could taste some intangible yet exceptional quality.

We kept patching and then repatching the ragged-ass fence, lacing it back together with twine and scraps of rope, with ancient twists of baling wire, and with coat hangers; propping splintered shipping pallets against the gaps, stacking them and leaning them here and there in an attempt to plug the many holes. (The calves ended up merely using these pallets as ladders and springboards.)

In his own bedraggled state, however, Ben saw none of the failures. "That's what being a cattleman's about," he said — he who had never owned a cow in his life. "Ninety-five percent of it is the grunt work, and five percent is buying low and selling high. I like how you boys work at it," he said, and he never dreamed or knew that in our own half-assedness we were making much more work for ourselves than if we'd done the job right the first time.

After we got our driver's licenses we used Ben's old station wagon — he was no longer able to drive — and after getting him to bed, and hasping the doors shut as if stabling some wild horse, and latching the windows from the outside, we left the darkened farmhouse and headed for the lights of the city, which cast a golden half-dome high into the fog and scudding clouds.

It was a vast glowing ball of light, seeming close enough that we could have walked or ridden our bikes to reach it: and driving Ben's big station wagon, with its power steering and gas-sucking engine, was like piloting a rocket ship. There were no shades of gray, out in the country like that: there was only the quiet stillness of night, with crickets chirping, and fireflies, too, back then, and the instrument panels on the dashboard were the only light of fixed reference as we powered through that darkness, hungry for that nearing dome of city light. The gauges and dials before us were nearly as mysterious to us as the instrument panel of a jet airplane, and neither Moxley nor I paid much attention to them. For the most part, he knew only the basics: how to aim the car, steering it crudely like the iron gunboat it was, and how to use the accelerator and the brakes.

And after but a few miles of such darkness there would suddenly be light, blazes of it hurled at us from all directions — grids and window squares and spears of light, sundials and radials of influorescence and neon; and we were swallowed by it, were born into it, and suddenly we could see before us the hood of the old Detroit iron horse that had carried us into the city and swallowed us, as the city, and Westheimer Avenue, seemed to be swallowing the car, and we were no longer driving so much as being driven.

All-night gas stations, all-night grocery stores, movie theaters, restaurants, massage parlors, oil-change garages, floral shops, apartment complexes, dentists' offices, car dealerships — it was all jammed shoulder to shoulder, there was no zoning, and though we had seen it all before in the daytime, and were accustomed to it, it looked entirely different at night: alluring, even beautiful, rather than squalid and chaotic.

The neon strip fascinated us, as might a carnival, but what ultimately caught our imagination on these night sojourns was not the glamorous, exotic urban core but the strange seams of disintegrating roughness on the perimeters, pockets toward and around which the expanding city spilled and flowed like lava: little passed-by islands of the past, not unlike our own on the western edge. We passed through the blaze of light and strip malls, the loneliness of illuminated commerce, and came out the other side, on the poorer eastern edge, where all the high-voltage power grids were clustered, and the multinational refineries.

Here the air was dense with the odor of burning plastic, vaporous benzenes and toluenes adhering to the palate with every breath, and the night-fog sky glowed with blue, pink, orange flickers from the flares of waste gas jetting from a thousand smokestacks. The blaze of commerce faded over our shoulders and behind us, and often we found ourselves driving through neighborhoods that seemed to be sinking into the black soil, the muck of peat, as if pressed down by the immense weight of the industrial demands placed upon that spongy soil — gigantic tanks and water towers and chemical vats, strange intestinal folds and coils of tarnished aluminum towering above us, creeping through the remnant forests like nighttime serpents.

Snowy egrets and night herons passed through the flames, or so it seemed, and floated amid the puffs of pollution as serenely as if in a dream of grace; and on those back roads, totally lost, splashing through puddles axle deep and deeper, and thudding over potholes big enough to hold a bowling ball, Moxley would sometimes turn the lights off and navigate the darkened streets in that manner, passing through pools of rainbow-colored poisonous light and wisps and tatters of toxic fog, as if gliding with the same grace and purpose as the egrets above us. Many of the rotting old homes had ancient live oaks out in front, their yards bare due to the trees' complete shading of the soil. In the rainy season, the water stood a foot deep in the streets, so that driving up and down them was more like poling the canals of Venice than driving; and the heat from our car's undercarriage hissed steam as we plowed slowly up and down.

We were drawn to these rougher, ranker places at night, and yet we wanted to see them in the full light of day also; and when we traveled to these eastern edges during school, while taking a long lunch break or cutting classes entirely, we discovered little hanging-on businesses run out of those disintegrating houses, places where old men and women still made tortillas by hand, or repaired leather boots and work shoes, or did drywall masonry, or made horseshoes by hand, even though there were increasingly few horses and ever more cars and trucks, especially trucks, as urban Texas began the calcification of its myths in full earnestness.

Places where a patch of corn might exist next to a ten-story office building, places where people still hung their clothes on the line to dry, and little five- and ten-acre groves in which there might still exist a ghost-herd of deer. Ponds in which there might still lurk giant, sullen, doomed catfish, even with the city's advancing hulk blocking now partially the rising and setting of the sun.

Through such explorations we found the Goat Man as surely and directly as if he had been standing on the roof of his shed, calling to us with some foxhunter's horn, leading us straight to the hand-painted rotting plywood sign tilted in the mire outside his hovel.

BABY CLAVES, $15, read the sign, each letter painted a different color, as if by a child. We parked in his muddy driveway, the low-slung station wagon dragging its belly over the corrugated troughs of countless such turnings-around, wallowing and slithering and splashing up to the front porch of a collapsing clapboard shed-house that seemed to be held up by nothing more than the thick braids and ghost vines of dead ivy.

Attached to the outside of the hovel was a jerry-built assemblage of corrals and stables, ramshackle slats of mixed-dimension scrap lumber, from behind which came an anguished cacophony of bleats and bawls and whinnies and outright bloodcurdling screams, as we got out of the car and sought to make our way dry-footed from one mud hummock to the next, up toward the sagging porch, to inquire about the baby claves, hoping very much that they were indeed calves, and not some odd bivalve oyster we'd never heard of.

We peered through dusty windows (some of the panes were cracked, held together with fraying duct tape) and saw that many of the rooms were filled with tilted mounds of newspapers so ancient and yellowing that they had begun to turn into mulch.

An old man answered the door when we knocked, the man blinking not so much as if having been just awakened but as if instead rousing himself from some other communion or reverie, some lost-world voyage. He appeared to be in his sixties, with a long wild silver beard and equally wild silver hair, in the filaments of which fluttered a few moths, as if he were an old bear that had just been roused from his work of snuffling through a rotting log in search of grubs.

His teeth were no better than the slats that framed the walls of his ragged corrals, and, barefoot, he was dressed in only a pair of hole-sprung, oil-stained forest green workpants, on which we recognized the dried-brown flecks of manure splatter, and an equally stained sleeveless ribbed underwear T-shirt that had once been white but was now the color of his skin, and appeared to have been on his body so long as to become like a second kind of skin — one that, if it were ever removed, might peel off with it large patches of his original birth skin.

The odor coming from the house was quite different from the general barnyard stench of feces, and somehow even more offensive.

Despite the general air of filth and torpor radiating from the house and its host, however, his carriage and bearing were erect, almost military — as if our presence had electrified him with hungry possibility; as if we were the first customers, or potential customers, he might have encountered in so long a time that he had forgotten his old patterns of defeat.

When he first spoke, however, to announce his name, the crispness of his posture was undercut somewhat by the shining trickle of tobacco drool that escaped through some of the gaps in his lower teeth, like a slow release of gleaming venom.

"Sloat," he said, and at first I thought it was some language of his own making: that he was attempting to fix us, tentatively, with a curse. "Heironymous Sloat," he said, reaching out a gnarly spittle- and mucus-stained hand. We exchanged looks of daring and double-daring, and finally Moxley offered his own pale and unscarred hand.

"Come in," Sloat said, making a sweeping gesture that was both grand and familial — as if, horrifically, he recognized in us some kindred spirit — and despite our horror, after another pause, we followed him in.

Since all the other rooms were filled with newspapers and tin cans, Sloat's bed had been dragged into the center room. The kitchen was nearly filled with unwashed pots and dishes, in which phalanxes of roaches stirred themselves into sudden scuttling escape as we entered. The rug in the center room was wet underfoot — the water-stained, sagging ceiling was still dripping from the previous night's rain, and on the headboard of the bed there was a small fishbowl, filled with cloudy water, in which a goldfish hung suspended, slowly finning in place, with nothing else in the bowl but a single short decaying sprig of seaweed.

The fish's water was so cloudy with its own befoulment as to seem almost viscous, and for some reason the fish so caught my attention that I felt hypnotized, suspended in the strange house — as if I had become the fish. I had no desire to move, and neither could I look anywhere else. All of my focus was on that one little scrap of color, once bright but now muted, though still living.

I glanced over at Moxley and was disturbed to see that he seemed somehow invigorated, even stimulated, by the rampant disorder.

So severe was my hypnosis, and so disoriented were both of us, that neither of us had noticed there was someone sleeping in the rumpled, unmade bed beside which we stood; and when the person stirred, we stepped back, alarmed.

The sleeper was a young woman, not much older than we were, sleeping in a nightgown only slightly less dingy than the shirt of the older man — and though it was midafternoon, and bright outside, her face was puffy with sleep, and she stirred with such languor that I felt certain she had been sleeping all day.

She sat up and stared at us as if trying to make sense of us, and brushed her hair from her shoulders. Her hair was orange, very nearly the same color as the fish's dull scales, and

Sloat stared at her in a way that was both dismissive and yet slightly curious — as if wondering why, on this day, she had awakened so early.

She swung her feet off the bed and stood unsteadily, and watched us with unblinking raptness.

"Let's go look at the stock," Sloat said, and we could tell that it gave him pleasure to say the word *stock*.

The three of us went through the cluttered kitchen and out to the backyard — it surprised me that there were no dogs or cats in the house — and the girl followed us to the door but no farther, and stood there, on the other side of the screen. Her bare feet, I had noticed, were dirty, as if she had made the journey out to the stables before, but on this occasion lingered behind, perhaps made shy.

Sloat was wearing old sharp-toed cowboy boots, his thin shanks shoved into them in such a way that I knew he wasn't wearing socks, and he walked in a brisk, almost fierce line straight through the puddles and troughs toward the stables, as if he enjoyed splashing through the muck and grime, while Moxley and I pussyfooted from little hummock to hummock, sometimes slipping and dipping a foot in one water-filled rut or another. Whitish foam floated on the top of many of the puddles, as if someone, or something, had been urinating in them.

Sloat pushed through a rickety one-hinge gate, and goats, chickens, and other fleeting, unidentified animals scattered before his explosive entrance. Sloat began cursing and shouting at them, then picked up a stick and rat-tat-tatted it along the pickets to excite them further, like a small boy, and as if to demonstrate their vigor to their potential buyers.

A pig, a pony, a rooster. A calf, or something that looked like a calf, except for its huge head, which was so out of proportion for the tiny body that it seemed more like the head of an elephant.

"I buy them from the Feist brothers," he said. "The ones that don't get sold at auction. They give me a special deal," he said.

The animals continued to bleat and caterwaul, flowing away, flinging themselves against the fences. Some of them ran in demented circles, and others tried to burrow in the mud, while the goats, the most nimble of them, leapt to the tops of the little crude-hammered, straw-lined doghouses and peered down with their wildly disconcerting vertical-slit lantern green eyes as if welcoming Moxley and me into some new and alien fraternity of half man, half animal: and as if, now that Moxley and I were inside the corral, the goats had us exactly where they wanted us.

Moxley had eyes only for the calves, thin-ribbed though they were, dehydrated and listless, almost sleepwalkerish compared to the frenzy and exodus of the other animals. Six of them were huddled over in one corner of the makeshift corral, quivering collectively, their stringy tails and flanks crusted green.

"Which are the fifteen-dollar ones?" he asked, and, sensing weakness, Sloat replied, "Those are all gone now. The only ones I have left are thirty-five."

Moxley paused. "What about that little Brahma?" he asked, pointing to the one animal that was clearly superior, perhaps even still healthy.

"Oh, that's my little prize bull," Sloat said. "I couldn't let you have him for less than seventy-five."

Between us, we had only sixty-five, which in the end turned out to be precisely enough. We had no trailer attached to the back of the station wagon, but Sloat showed us how we could pull out the back seat, lash the seat to the roof for the drive home, and line the floor and walls of the station wagon with squares of cardboard, in case the calf soiled it, and drive home with him in that manner. "I've done it many a time myself," Sloat said.

The girl had come out to watch us, had waded barefoot through the same puddles in which her father, or whatever his relation was to her, had waded. She now stood on the other side of the gate, still wearing her nightgown, and watched us as Sloat and Moxley and I, our financial transaction completed, chased the bull calf around the corral, slipping in the muck, Sloat swatting the calf hard with a splintered baseball bat, whacking it whenever he could, and Moxley and me trying to tackle the calf and wrestle it to the ground.

The calf was three times as strong as any one of us, however, and time and again no sooner had one of us gotten a headlock on it than it would run into the side of the corral, smashing the would-be tackler hard against the wall; and soon both Moxley and I were bleeding from our shins, noses, and foreheads, and I had a split lip — and still Sloat kept circling the corral, following the terrified calf, smacking him hard with the baseball bat.

Somehow, all the other creatures had disappeared — had vanished into other, adjacent corrals, or perhaps through a maze of secret passageways — and, leaning against one of the wobbly slat walls, blood dripping from my nose, I saw now what Sloat had been doing with his wild tirade: that each time the calf rounded a corner, Sloat had pushed open another gap or gate and ushered two or three more nontarget animals into one of the outlying pens, until finally the calf was isolated.

Sloat was winded, and he stood there gasping and sucking air, the bat held loosely in his hands. The calf stood facing the three of us, panting likewise, and suddenly Sloat rushed him, seemingly having waited to gauge when the animal would be midbreath, too startled or tired to bolt, and he struck the calf as hard as he could with the baseball bat, striking it on the bony plate of its forehead.

The calf neither buckled nor wobbled, but seemed only to sag a little, as if for a long time he had been tense or worried about something but could now finally relax.

Sloat hit the calf again quickly, and then a third and fourth time, striking it now like a man trying to hammer a wooden stake into the ground, and that was how the calf sank, shutting its eyes and folding, sinking lower; and still Sloat kept striking it as if he intended to punish it or kill it, or both.

He did not stop until the calf was unconscious, or perhaps dead, and lying on its side. Then he laid his bat down almost tenderly — as if it were some valuable instrument to be accorded great respect.

The Goat Girl watched as if she had seen it all before. Sloat paused to catch his breath and then called to us to help him heft the calf quickly, before it came back to consciousness, though we could not imagine such a thing, and I was thinking at first that he had just stolen our money: had taken our sixty-five dollars, killed our calf, and was now demanding our assistance in burying it.

The Goat Girl roused herself finally, and she splashed through the puddles of foam and slime, out toward the car in advance of us, as if intending to lay palm fronds before our approach, and she opened our car door and placed the scraps of cardboard in the car's interior, for when the calf resurrected.

"How long will he be out?" Moxley asked.

"Where are you taking him?" Sloat asked, and I told him, *West Houston* — about an hour and a half away.

"An hour and a half," said Sloat, whom I had now begun to think of as the Goat Man. He shook our proffered hands — cattlemen! — and told us, as we were driving off, to come back soon, that he had a lot of volume coming through, and that he would keep an eye out for good stock, for buyers as discerning as we were, and that he would probably be able to give us a better break next time.

Moxley slithered the station wagon out to the end of the drive — the Goat Man and Goat Girl followed — and Moxley stopped and rolled his window down and thanked them both again and asked the girl what her name was.

But she had fallen into a reverie and was staring at us in much the same manner as the calf had after receiving his first blow; and as we drove away she did not raise her hand to return our waves, and neither did she give any other sign of having seen or heard us, or that she was aware of our existence in the world.

Driving away, I was troubled deeply by the ragtag, slovenly, almost calculated half-assedness of the operation; and on the drive home, though Moxley and I for the most part were pleased and excited about having gotten another calf, and so cheaply, I was discomforted, could feel a rumbling confusion, the protest that sometimes precedes revolution though other times leads to nothing, only acquiescence, then senescence. I could see that Moxley did not feel it — and, sensing this, I felt weaker, and slightly alone.

The calf woke up when we were still an hour from Ben's ranch. The calf did not awaken gradually, as a human might, stirring and blinking and looking around to ascertain his new surroundings, but awoke instead explosively, denting a crumple in the roof immediately with his bony head. He squealed and then began crashing against the sides of the car's interior so violently, and with such a clacking of hoofs, that we were afraid he would break the glass and escape; and his frenzied thrashings (he was unable to stand to his full height in the back of the car, and instead began crawling) reminded me of how, hours earlier, the calf had been rounding the makeshift corral.

We attempted to shoo the calf to the back, swatting at him with our hands, but these gestures held no more meaning for the bull than if we had been waving flyswatters at him, and his squeals transformed to full roars, amplified to terrifying proportions within the confines of the car. At one point he was in the front seat with us, having lunged over it, and in his flailings managed to head-butt me, and he cut Moxley's shins so deeply with swift kicks of his sharp little hoofs that they were bruised and bleeding, and he nearly ran off the road — but then the calf decided it preferred the space and relative freedom of the back seat and vaulted back over the seat again and into its cardboard lair, where it continued to hurl itself against the walls.

As the Goat Man had foreseen, and as a symptom of the ailment that had caused it to not be bid upon in the first place at the regular auction — the auction that had preceded the mysterious Feist brothers' obtaining him — the calf in its fright began emitting fountains of greenish, watery diarrhea, spraying it midwhirl as if from a hose, so that we were yelling and ducking, and soon the interior of the car was nearly coated with dripping green slime. And though panicked, we were fierce in our determination to see this thing through, and we knew that if we stopped and turned the calf out into the open, we would never capture it again.

Somehow we made it home, and in the darkness of the new evening, with fireflies blinking in the fields, we drove straight out into Old Ben's pasture, ghostly gray weeds scraping and scratching against the sides of the wagon with an eerie, clawing keen that further terrified the calf: and when we rolled down the tailgate's window he leapt out into that clean sweet fresh night air; and this calf, too, we never saw again, though the residue of his journey, his passage, remained with us for weeks afterward, in cracks and crevices of the old station wagon, despite our best scrubbing.

Old Ben fell further into the rot. Moxley and I could both see it, in his increasing lapses of memory, and his increasingly erratic behavior; and though I had perceived Moxley to be somehow more mature than I — more confident in the world — I was surprised by how vulnerable Moxley seemed to be made by Ben's fading.

Ben was ancient, a papery husk of a man — dusty, tottering history, having already far exceeded the odds by having lived as long as he had — and was going downhill fast. Such descent could not be pleasant for Old Ben, who, after all, had once been a young man much like ourselves. His quality of life was plummeting even as ours, fueled by the strength of our youth, was ascending. Did Moxley really expect, or even want, for the old man to hang on forever, an eternal hostage to his failed and failing body, just so Moxley would have the luxury of having an older surviving family member?

We couldn't keep him locked up all the time. Moxley had taken over control of the car completely, took it to school each day, and hid the keys whenever he was home, but Old

Ben's will was every bit as fierce as Moxley's, and Ben continued to escape. We often found him floating in the stock tank,
using an inner tube for a life vest, fishing, with no hook tied
to his line, flailing at the water determinedly.

He disappeared for a week once after rummaging through
the drawers and finding the key to the tractor, which he
drove away, blowing a hole through the back wall of the
barn. We didn't notice the hole, or that the tractor was miss-
ing, and it was not until a sheriff called from Raton County,
New Mexico, asking if Moxley knew an elderly gentleman
named Ben, before we had any clue of where he was. We
skipped school and drove out there to get him, pulling a
rented flatbed on which to strap the tractor, and he was as
glad to see us as a child would have been; and Moxley, in his
relief, was like a child himself, his eyes tearing with joy.

All through that winter we continued to buy more stock
from the Goat Man, knowing better but unable to help ourselves, and lured, too, by the low prices. Even if one in ten
of his scour-ridden wastrels survived to market, we would
come out ahead, we told ourselves, but none of them did:
they all escaped through our failed fence, usually in the very
first afternoon of their freedom, and we never saw any of
them again.

We imagined their various fates. We envisioned certain of
them being carried away by the panthers that were rumored
to still slink through the Brazos river bottoms, and the black
jaguars that were reported to have come up from Mexico,
following those same creeks and rivers as if summoned, to
snack on our cheap and ill-begotten calves, or *claves*, as we
called them. We imagined immense gargoyles and winged
harpies that swooped down to snatch up our renegade run-

away crops. We envisioned modern-day cattle rustlers congregating around the perimeter of our ranch like fishermen. It was easy to imagine that even the Goat Man himself followed us home and scooped up each runaway calf in a net, and returned with it then to his lair, where he would sell it a second time to another customer.

Or perhaps there was some hole in the earth, some cavern into which all the calves disappeared, as if sucked there by a monstrous and irresistible force. Any or all of these paranoias might as well have been true, given the completeness of the calves' vanishings.

With each purchase we made I felt more certain that we were traveling down a wrong path, and yet we found ourselves returning to the Goat Man's hovel again and again, and giving him more and more money.

We ferried our stock in U-Haul trailers, and across the months, as we purchased more cowflesh from the Goat Man — meat vanishing into the ether again and again, as if into some quarkish void — we became familiar enough with Sloat and his daughter to learn that her name was Flozelle, and to visit with them about matters other than stock.

We would linger in that center room — bedroom, dining room, living room, all — and talk briefly, first about the weather and then about the Houston Oilers, before venturing out into what Moxley and I had taken to calling the Pissyard. We learned that Flozelle's mother had died when she was born, that Flozelle had no brothers or sisters, and that Sloat loathed schools.

"I homeschool her," he said. "Go ahead, ask her anything."

We could have been wiseasses. We could have flaunted our ridiculously little knowledge — the names of signatories to various historical documents, the critical dates of various armistices — but in the presence of such abject filth, and before her shell-shocked quietude, we were uncharacteristically humbled. Instead, Moxley asked, almost gently, "How long have you had that fish?" and before Flozelle could answer, Sloat bullshitted us by telling us that the fish had been given to his grandmother on her wedding day, almost a hundred years ago.

"What's its name?" I asked, and this time, before Sloat could reply, Flozelle answered.

"Goldy," she said proudly, and a shiver ran down my back. If I had known what sadness or loneliness really felt like, I think I might have recognized it as such; but as it was, I felt only a shiver, and then felt it again as she climbed up onto the unmade bed (the bottoms of her bare feet unwashed and bearing little crumb fragments) and unscrewed the lid to a jar of uncooked oatmeal she kept beside the bowl, and sprinkled a few flakes into the viscous water.

Moxley was watching her with what seemed to me to be a troubled look, and after she had finished feeding the bloated fish, she turned and climbed back down off the lumpen bed, and then we filed out through the kitchen and on out into the Pissyard to go look at, and purchase, more stock.

Back before Ben had begun falling to pieces, Moxley and I had sometimes gone by my house after school to do homework and hang out. My mother would make cookies, and if Moxley was still there when my father got home from work, Moxley would occasionally have supper with us. But those days had gone by long ago, Ben now requiring almost all of his waking care. I helped as I could, doing little things like cleaning up the house. Whenever Ben discovered that he was trapped he would ransack the house, pulling books down off shelves and hurling his clothes out of his drawer; once he rolled up the carpet and tried to set the end of it on fire, as if lighting a giant cigar: when we arrived at the farmhouse, we could see the toxic gray smoke seeping from the windows, and, rushing inside, we found Ben passed out next to the rug, which had smoldered and burned a big hole in the plywood flooring, revealing the gaping maw of dark basement below, with the perimeter of that burned-out crater circular, like a caldera, having burned so close to Ben that his left arm hung down into the pit. All the next day we hammered and sawed new sheets of plywood to patch that abyss. For a few days afterward, Ben seemed contrite and neither misbehaved nor otherwise suffered any departures from sentience, as if such lapses had been, after all, at least partially willful.

I helped cook dinners, and some nights I stayed over at their farmhouse and helped make breakfast, and helped Moxley batten down the doors and windows before leaving for school. Knives, scissors, matches, guns, fishhooks, lighter fluid, gasoline, household cleaners — it all had to be put away. Moxley had tied a 150-foot length of rope around Ben's waist each night so that if Ben awoke and went sleepwalking, wandering the dewy hills, he could be tracked and reeled in like a marlin or other sport fish.

The farmhouse was a pleasant place to awaken in the morning — the coppery sun rising just above the tops of the trees, and the ungrazed fields lush and tall and green, with mourning doves cooing and pecking red grit and gravel from the driveway — and the interior of the house would be spangled with the prisms of light from all the little pieces of glass arrayed on the windowsill, Ben's shrapnel collection. The spectral casts of rainbow would be splashed all over the walls, like the light that passes through stained-glass windows, and there would be no sound but the ticking of the grandfather clock in the front hallway, and the cooing of those doves, and the lowing of distant cows not ours. Moxley and I would fix breakfast, gather our homework, then lock up the house and leave, hurrying toward school.

I had some money from mowing lawns, and Moxley was pretty flush, or so it seemed to us, from Ben's pension checks. As much from habit now as from desire, we made further pilgrimages to Sloat's corrals that winter and spring.

And following each purchase, upon our return to Ben's ranch, sometimes our new crop of sickly calves would remain in the pasture for a few days, though never longer than a week, after which, always, they disappeared, carrying with them their daunting and damnable genes, the strange double-crossed combination of recessive alleles that had caused the strangeness to blossom in them in the first place — the abnormality, the weakness, that had led to the unfortunate chain of circumstances that resulted in their passing from a real auction to the Feist brothers, who would sell them for dog meat if they could, and then to Sloat and a short life of squalor, and then to us, and then to whatever freedom or destiny awaited them.

Ben caught pneumonia after one of his escapes. (He had broken out a window and crawled through, leaving a trail of blood as well as new glass scattered amid his sparkling windowsill shards of glass from fifty years earlier; we trailed him down to the pond, his favorite resting spot, where he stood shivering, waist deep, as if awaiting a baptism.) Moxley had to check him into the hospital, and after he was gone the silence in the farmhouse was profound.

Moxley was edgy, waiting for the day when Old Ben would be coming home, but that day never came; he would die in the hospital. And although it had long been clear that Ben's days at home were numbered, the abyss of his final absence still came as a surprise, as did Moxley's new anger.

We continued with our old rituals, as if Ben was still with us — cooking the steaks on the back porch grill, and buying cattle — but the ground beneath our feet seemed less firm.

With Old Ben's last pension check Moxley and I went to a real auction and bought a real calf — not one of Sloat's misfits, but a registered Brahma — a stout little bull calf. And rather than risk losing this one, we kept it tethered, like a dog on a leash, in the barn. It was not as wild as Sloat's terrified refugees, and soon we were able to feed and water it by hand: and it grew fatter, week by week. We fed it a diet rich in protein, purchasing sweet alfalfa and pellet cubes. We brushed it and curried it and estimated its weight daily as we fatted it for market. And it seemed to me that with some success having finally been achieved, Moxley's anger and loneliness had stabilized, and I was glad that this calf, at least, had not escaped. It was a strange thought to both of us, to consider that we were raising the animal so someone else could eat him, but that was what cattlemen did.

As this calf, finally, grew fatter, Moxley seemed to grow angry at the Goat Man, and barely spoke to him now when we traveled out there; and though we still went out there with the same, if not greater, frequency, we had stopped purchasing stock from the Goat Man and instead merely went out into the Pissyard to look. After we had purchased the calf from the regular auction, Sloat's offerings were revealed to us in their full haplessness and we could not bring ourselves to take them at any price; still, we went to look, almost morbidly curious about what misfits might have passed through his gates that week.

Moxley asked Flozelle out on what I suppose could be labeled a date, even though I was with them. I wanted to believe the best of him, but it seemed to me that there was a meanness, a bedevilment. Moxley still had the same aspirations — he was intent on going to school and becoming a vet — but the moments of harshness seemed to emerge from him at odd and unpredictable times, like fragments of bone or glass emerging from beneath the thinnest of skin.

The three of us began to ride places together once or twice a week, and, for a while, she fascinated us. She knew how to fix things — how to rebuild a carburetor, how to peel a tire from its rim and plug it with gum and canvas and seat it back onto its rim again — and sometimes, out in the country, we stopped beside the fields of strangers and got out and climbed over the barbed-wire fence and went out to where other people's horses were grazing. We would slip up onto those horses bareback and ride them around strangers' fields for hours at a time. Flozelle knew how to gentle even the most unruly or skittish horse by biting its ears with her teeth and hanging on like a pit bull until Moxley or I had climbed up, and then she'd release her bite hold and we'd rocket across the pasture, the barrel ribs of the horse beneath us heaving; the expensive thoroughbreds of oilmen, the sleek and fatted horses farting wildly from their too rich diets of grain.

She had never been to a movie before, and when we took her she stared rapt, ate three buckets of popcorn, chewing ceaselessly through *Star Wars*. She began spending some afternoons with Moxley out at his farm, and helping him with chores — mowing with the tractor the unkempt grass, bush-hogging brush and cutting bales of hay for our young bull. She showed us how to castrate him, to make him put on even more weight even faster, and she set about repairing the shabby, sorry fence we had never gotten around to fixing properly.

The calf, the steer, was getting immense, or so it seemed to us, and though he still was friendly and manageable, his strength concerned us. We worried that he might strangle himself on his harness, his leash, should he ever attempt to break out of the barn, and so not long after Flozelle had completed her repairs on the fence we turned him out into the field, unfastening his rope and opening the barn doors, whereupon he emerged slowly, blinking, and then descended to the fresh green fields below and began grazing there confidently, as if he had known all his life that those fields were waiting for him, and that he would reach them in due time.

I had the strange thought that if only Old Ben could have still been alive to see it, the sight might somehow have helped heal him, even though I knew that to be an impossibility. He had been an old man, war torn and at the end of his line; no amount of care, or even miracles, could have kept him from going downhill.

To the best of my knowledge, Flozelle did not shower, as if such a practice went against her or her father's religious beliefs. In my parents' car I drove up to the farm one warm day in the spring, unannounced, and surprised Moxley and Flozelle, who were out in the backyard. Moxley was dressed but Flozelle was not, and Moxley was spraying her down with the hose — not in fun, as I might have suspected, but in a manner strangely more workmanlike, as one might wash a car, or even a horse; and when they saw me Moxley was embarrassed and shut the hose off, though Flozelle was not discomfited at all, and merely took an old towel, little larger than a washcloth, and began drying off.

And later, after he had taken her back home — after we had both driven out to Sloat's and dropped her off, without going inside, and without going back into the Pissyard to look around, I asked him, "Are you sleeping with her?" — and he looked at me with true surprise and then said, "I am," and when I asked him if she ever spent the night over at the farmhouse, he looked less surprised, less proud, and said yes.

What did it matter to me? It was nothing but an act, almost lavatory-like in nature, I supposed — almost mechanical and without emotion, if not insensate. I imagined it to be for Moxley like the filling of a hole, the shoveling-in of something, and the tamping-down. It was not anything. He was doing what he had to do, almost as if taking care of her; and she, with all the things the Goat Man had taught her, had fixed his fences, had repaired the old tractor, the barn.

She had not led him down any errant path, and neither was his life, or mine, going to change or deviate from our destinies as a result of any choices made or not made. She was like fodder, was all. We were just filling the days. We were still fattening up. We were still strong in the world, and moving forward. I had no call to feel lonely or worried. We still had all the time in the world, the world was still ours, there was no rot anywhere, the day was still fresh and new, we could do no wrong. We would grow, just not now.

PENETRATIONS

MY OLDER BROTHER, Sam, was a ladies' man. When I was seventeen, he was twenty-two, and during my junior year of high school, to my great initial horror, he began dating my biology teacher, Miss Heathcote, and then, worse yet, fell in love with her, and, worst of all, she fell in love with him. I asked Sam to try to keep it a secret from her that I was his brother, because I was worried that it might make trouble for me in class.

My brother was not right — and though he is better today, has been treated and has also straightened up some, I still fear that a rough road lies ahead of him. But back then he was only beginning to go wrong, to unravel — to feel ungoverned by any laws or constraints.

Sam lived at home, with my parents and me. He had been a fireman for a while but had been let go from the force for "general irresponsibility"; the fire department had believed that he had almost a fetish for danger, for daring.

Sam had wanted to be a policeman after that, but he had a couple of shoplifting convictions, and that was out of the question. I think he would very much have enjoyed being a policeman.

I do not mean to make him sound like such a renegade. He was a good brother, and even today we're still close. He has been married and divorced once. He's never gotten into any kind of legal trouble, since he was eighteen. Both times, back then, he tried to walk out of a store with a coat — mink, the first time, and lynx, the next — for his girlfriends, on a dare. The same security guard who had caught him the first time was on duty the second time — Sam wearing the coat as if it were a Windbreaker, and as if it were his, walking then sprinting for the doorway in his jeans and tennis shoes.

I remember my parents' being distressed that Sam was drifting off on a wrong course — they were not so wild about him living at home either, though as I heard my father say once, "Better here, at least, where we can keep an eye on him" — but back then I did not recognize so well that it was a wrong course, and I simply enjoyed being around the danger of Sam, or, rather, the way Sam was drawn to danger, and to heat.

What Sam did when he was twenty-two, besides courting women (and women loved him), was to chase ambulances and fire trucks, after the fire department let him go. Sam had a police scanner radio in his room, and another mounted beneath the dash in his truck, and fire extinguishers in the back of the truck. I don't mean three or four fire extinguishers, but a whole truckload. He had purchased them, he said, from the fire department at "a substantial discount," and he used them at will.

Sam wore a fire chief's helmet, which he would don whenever any of the calls went out. He had a city map in the glove box, which he studied all the time. He would listen to the scanners and try to get to the scenes of disaster before anyone else — before the authorities — and sometimes he was successful.

Occasionally, I went with him. Sam and I had certain rules, when we went out on fire calls, and we had, on the times that we could not get there in time to be the heroes, invented a game that we called Penetrations. The object was to see how close to the center of the disaster you could get, or "penetrate" — to go from the outside, and the ring of spectators, into the center, so that you were part of whatever was happening — so that you were as close to it as you could be, so that you could reach out and touch it, if you wanted.

If a home was burning, we would try to get inside it — we would pretend it was our house, and that we'd left something valuable inside. When the firemen grabbed us, we'd put on an act, pitch a fit, and struggle to break free; so close to the inferno that we could feel the wind from the fire, so close that the heat blistered our bare faces. Sometimes we got close enough to actually touch the front door. We never made it inside a burning building, but we tried; for whatever crazy reason, Sam tried, and I followed him: I tried, too. We never got in, though; there was always someone to restrain us and keep us from going any farther. I don't know how far we really would have gone. We never really found out.

Miss Heathcote was thirty-two or thirty-three, and beautiful. She was the only attractive teacher in the school, and as such was always an outcast, away from the other teachers. The women were distant or catty to her — even then we could see that, and knew it for what it was — and the men were worse: they were fawning, slobbering pigs, coming around her all the time like animals checking out a trough. There was the delicious and wild rumor that Miss Heathcote had been a Playmate in her younger days, in that magazine, and there was not a student among us who did not believe it, or who had not researched the rumor, though no such issue was ever produced — but we knew it was out there, in the past, we could picture it as clear as day, until in our minds we believed that maybe we *had* seen it but had just misplaced it . . .

Sam and I managed to keep the fact that we were brothers a secret for about three weeks before Miss Heathcote found out. She came over to the house one afternoon and I simply forgot to hide — it suddenly seemed natural to me, to be sitting there out in the open — and though she was a little annoyed with Sam about having kept it a secret, she didn't take it out on me. In fact, she was gentle and kind with me. Some mornings the three of us would have coffee and doughnuts together, before driving to school — and so that made me feel bad about what I told my classmates.

"On weekends, when my parents are out, she comes over and swings from the chandeliers naked," I told them. "She pulled one out of the ceiling once."

Such tales were easily believable in the heat of our adolescence, and I made up worse ones than that. I simply couldn't help it. We would sit there in class and watch her calm beauty — the startling depth of her eyes, and the deep, relaxed peace she cast over us — as she murmured the complexities of biology, telling them to us like a fairy tale rather than a hard science, and these things seemed only to enhance the stories I made up about her.

Her placidness, her great gentleness, seemed certain to suggest a raging, lusty inferno lying just below the surface, a surface as thin as ice. She'd been at the school for ten years, the only school she'd ever taught at (Sam had gone to a private boys' school, sort of a disciplinarian retreat, when he was my age).

The students, always hungry, believed the stories I made up about Miss Heathcote and Sam as they had never believed anything before.

My parents were not much older than Miss Heathcote — they were in their midforties — and were a little uncomfortable, at first, not knowing whether to treat her as a friend or as a friend of Sam's; but I'd heard them talking about her and Sam, when Sam and Miss Heathcote were out.

"She's a calm glass of water," my mother kept saying, " exactly what he needs," to which my father always replied, illogically, it seemed to me, "She's a beauty, all right" — and by Thanksgiving it felt as if Miss Heathcote were a part of our family. We were all comfortable with her — Sam, too, I think — in a way that we had never been comfortable with his other girlfriends.

Sometimes, after a fire or an accident, Sam and I would drive by Miss Heathcote's house. We'd circle the block again and again. She lived in the same house she had bought when she first moved to town, ten years ago. So beautiful, and never married! We'd cruise past that small house as if she were a teenager. Whenever any of my brother's old girlfriends called, he had instructed me, if I answered the phone I would tell them he wasn't home — tell them he'd moved away, tell them he'd died, tell them anything.

Frequently, he and Miss Heathcote went on picnics. I

rarely went on any of them, but on Friday nights I would watch him packing their lunches into the wicker basket, getting everything ready, and I could imagine what the picnics were like. Sam owned a canoe, with only one paddle, and he took her out in the early days of spring. I would picture Miss Heathcote lying back in the canoe, watching Sam paddle. I think I was in love with Miss Heathcote, too, a little, and I was afraid Sam was going to botch it.

Still, I could not help but continue to tell stories about her. Horrible, awful stories that stir me to shame, even now. "She dances in the street, naked, at night," I said. "The neighbors turn on their lights and look out their windows and watch. She's a good dancer," I added.

I knew that some of these stories were getting back to Miss Heathcote — I knew that they *had* to be — and she would look at me, sometimes, over at our house, a look passing between her and me, a look not in any way for Sam, a look that told me she knew, and that she did not like it at all; but she was so in love with Sam — forever holding his hand, forever running her hand through his hair as if trying to calm him, the way a man or woman might try to gentle a nervous horse in a burning barn, with the smell of smoke just beginning to drift in — that she never said anything to me, not wanting to stir the waters, not wanting to rock the boat. I think she thought that if she was nice enough to me, and gentle enough, that she could calm me, too, and that I would grow weary of creating the rumors, and I think, too, that she simply had too much pride to admit that she knew, or that it bothered her; and gradually, as the year went on, I did slow down on the stories, though I could still be counted on by my classmates, when pressured, to come up with a good one.

Something I *had* seen, which I did not tell the class, haunted me then, and still does. One time, back before he was fired, when Sam had to go to the fire station, she begged him not to; she wrapped her arms around his leg and wouldn't let him go. They weren't fighting — not yet she just didn't want him to go. Sam didn't know what to do. He loved his job and he had to get to the fire station. I had never seen such a thing: a woman trying *physically* to restrain a man from doing something. It seemed to me that Miss Heathcote's cool blue eyes, that her authority, would have been enough, but it wasn't. Sam left her and went out the door. I did not tell that story in school.

She was so much like family, that spring. I could not be around her enough; I wanted to spend all of my time in her company. Late nights, when she and Sam were in the den, watching the blue light of the TV, with both of my parents asleep upstairs, I would sometimes crawl on my belly down the hallway to get closer to Sam and Miss Heathcote, and to listen to them.

"This is what I do," I heard Miss Heathcote saying one time. "It's all I've learned to do, it's all I know. It's too late to change." She was lying in Sam's arms, and neither of them was watching the television. Their faces were blue, their arms.

"You *can* change!" Sam said softly. "Come with me to . . . oh . . . *Africa!*"

I was startled, and did not want Sam to leave, to go to Africa, or anywhere.

Miss Heathcote said nothing, but her shoulders began to heave and I could see her shaking her head, and I could see

big tears rolling down her cheeks as she continued to shake
her head.

Later in the spring, they would have fights. I wanted to
patch things, to mend them, to tell Miss Heathcote to hold
herself together, that Sam was difficult, but worth it, that he
was wonderful, that he saved people — but I could say none
of these things, because I had been telling lies about her, and
she would have no reason to believe me.

Back before he had even become a fireman, Sam and I put
out a house fire once, a kitchen blaze — the cabinets above
the stove flaming, and the rug on fire, the woman and her
two daughters out on the front lawn — and another time
we put out a car that was on fire. There wasn't anyone in
it, though at the time we thought there might be, and we
worked furiously, spraying the extinguishers, one after the
other, all over the car's melting body. The tires were explod-
ing, one by one, and the paint and rubber were smoking, filling the night with a horrible stench, and the car was long-
ago ruined, but we managed to get the fire put out before the
gas tank blew.

Other times, however — most times — we would get there
late. The ambulance would have arrived, and a sheet would
already be drawn over the victim, or the building would
already be in high flames, second-story flames, with sirens,
and hook-and-ladder trucks, flashing lights, fire hoses, and
loud speakers, bullhorns; and what we did then, which was
second-rate, and nowhere nearly as good as the other, but
the only thing we could manage, was to wander around
aimlessly on the lawn of the disaster, clasping our hands

over our heads and saying things like, "Oh, God" or "I'm wounded" — staggering around until one of the emergency technicians, not knowing us from the real victims, herded us over to the ambulance and sat us down, checked our pulse, checked our throats, our eyes, with flashlights, checked us for cuts, for burns, for bruises.

The questions were always the same — "Where does it hurt?" ("Aww, ohh, I don't know: here, I think") — and we'd lie around like that, getting attention, if no one else was seriously injured, and then, when the atmosphere started to change, when the chaos subsided and the fire was about to be controlled, or when the ambulance was about to pull away, we would leap up and run off into the night, and hide.

Our hearts would beat like rabbits'. The rest of our life was normal, and our parents never knew we did these things. I felt lucky to have such a brother.

"Are you okay, Jackie?" he'd ask me.

"Hell, yes," I'd say, still breathing hard.

"Good," he'd say, and I'd know he was proud of me, that we were partners. "Good."

We'd watch the flames coming out of the windows, watch the roof begin to crash and fall in, then, which is always how it happened: the roof going first. We felt noble; we felt as if we'd *tried* to save the burning house but had been unable to.

"We tried," I'd say.

"Fucking A," he'd agree, as if we'd been serious in our attempt. "We almost got there."

They were little fights between Sam and Miss Heathcote at first, but they grew. I didn't know what to do — I felt as if there were some act I could do, some gesture, that would bridge that gap, bridge their troubles; and the fights never grew from anything specific, never "I don't want to go there this evening" or "You told me that you were going to get a job," but rather just from vague fears, I think. They acted, both of them, all that spring, like skittish horses, nervous animals, each afraid to get any closer to the other — enjoying the other's company, devouring it, even, but hypnotized, it seemed, by the other: frightened.

I would answer the door when she came over to our house and knocked, and as I led her into the house I could actually *feel* her dread and her nervousness about the way things were going. Sam would be in his bedroom, working on electronic things, working on the police scanner, perhaps, or just listening to it, waiting for a disaster — because they were sure to happen; even in the slowest of weeks, it was simply a matter of listening, of lying there on the bed and waiting for one to happen — and the feeling I got when I led Miss Heathcote into the house was the feeling I might have gotten leading one of those same frightened horses *into* a burning stall — the smell of smoke — rather than out of it. Sometimes Miss Heathcote seemed near tears.

"I like her," I told Sam. "I sure do like her. Did she tell you I said mean things about her?"

"No," said Sam, looking up at the ceiling — looking up at nothing: there was nothing at all on the ceiling.

"She doesn't want me going out on fire calls," he said. He spoke to me as if I were an adult. "She doesn't like any of those things. She says she just wants to hold on to me and know those things are in me, just below the surface, but she doesn't want to see them." Sam lay there on his bed and looked up at the ceiling.

*

Even though they fought he would always try to calm her down, as she had once calmed him, running his hand down the back of her hair, rubbing her neck and shoulders, whispering things to her, reassuring things, as if trying to hypnotize her; but she always seemed to become even angrier than before, and it was an upsetting thing for me to see.

There was a gap between them — a small gap, but a significant one (even I could see that) — and later that spring, in May, with the school year nearing its end, and the possible loss of her to Sam also drawing nearer, I started playing Penetrations in class.

While Miss Heathcote had her back turned to us, writing on the blackboard — or sometimes even when she was facing us, head down, reading something, while we worked on an assignment — I would rise silently from my lab table and would begin walking to the front of the room — walking silently, slowly.

The object, in my mind, was to get as close in as I could before she noticed me. If she looked up, I would stop where I was. She would look at me, puzzled, but also abstracted — and I knew no one had ever behaved in such a fashion, that there were no guidelines in the teachers' handbook on how to deal with this oddity — and, strangely, she never said anything, only fixed me with her beautiful ice blue eyes and a strange, stern, almost steely look, watching me as if about to say something, but never saying it.

The class was as puzzled by her silence as I was. I pictured what it would be like if all of us played the Penetrations game — ten or twelve of us moving in on Miss Heathcote while her head was down, or her back turned, so that when she turned around there would be a whole herd of us, a dozen perhaps, frozen in midstep, all gathered around behind her — but it was something I was compelled to do, and something only I did, and perhaps that was why she let me do it: because she could see that I simply had to — or perhaps because she *liked* my doing it.

I never said anything when she looked up and stopped me in midstep — stopped me from getting any closer. I could never think of anything to say.

She would just open her mouth as if about to speak — but she never did.

I would walk up to within five or six feet of her, trying to see how close I could get before the lights of fear flickered in her eyes. Then I would stand there, quietly, trying to show her that it was all right, that there was nothing to be frightened of, but it never worked — she never lost that frightened look, once I had gotten too close — and finally I would go sit back down.

They were seeing each other more frequently than ever — Sam having lost his job by that time, and having extra time on his hands — and they went on more picnics, watched more movies, but fought more, too. It was all the same as it had been, only there was more of it. One Saturday they had the worst fight yet — Miss Heathcote crying and wrapping herself around Sam's waist again, sliding down to his legs, but then getting angry and getting up and throwing an ashtray and storming out of the house after that, slamming the door.

That Sunday, for the first time I could remember, she did not come over, and neither did Sam go over there. We stayed home, sat in his truck, and listened to a baseball game on the radio, and to the police scanner — and I thought it was over.

Then that Monday, during biology class, Sam showed up

at the window outside our room on the third floor. Sam was wearing his fireman's hat, and he had on his heavy rubber fireman's coat, and a hank of rope coiled over his shoulder; he was standing at the top of a ladder, tapping on the window, pointing to her. The class howled; they cheered. The windows were locked, but I got up and ran over and unlocked them; I was afraid Sam would fall.

When I opened the windows for Sam, Miss Heathcote looked at me as if she had always known it would be me who would betray her — that I would be the one — and she had that look, by the late spring, had it so well — I did not blame her — and Sam crawled gratefully through the window. He was wearing his boots, his rubber pants, his whole fireman's outfit. Miss Heathcote ran from him then, ran out of the classroom sobbing, and my brother followed, running in those high boots, calling her name. Several of the people in the class stood up to watch, and I felt myself swooning with excitement. He was my brother; he had chased our teacher from the room.

What happened after that, Sam would not tell and never has told me. He has been an alcoholic, and has recovered, lapsed, then recovered again; and he has had treatments for depression, and has gotten better. He's told me about all of those things and more; but he said the other things about what happened with Miss Heathcote were personal. He's held that tight to his breast, close to his coat, and told no one. It withers, it dies; the reasons for their fights, their breakup, almost do not even exist anymore.

These lives slide by, our lives! Sam is forty-three — my brother, forty-three. And Miss Heathcote — God, Miss Heathcote is well past half a century!

I remember Miss Heathcote smiling as she came up the

walk to go canoeing with my brother, and she really loved him, even if only briefly. And I think he made her feel things, for the first time in a while, I think — though, again, perhaps only briefly — and I hate to say this about my own brother, but I think she got off lucky.

I love Sam, but I think he would have made her really unhappy later in life. I think it — him and her together — would not have been a good idea: though who can say, for sure?

I remember going out with Sam on the fire calls, but even more I remember my own game of Penetrations that I played by myself, in class — rising and standing, and then beginning to move closer to her, slowly, carefully, trying to get close enough to touch her, to put my hand on her hand, perhaps, or even up against her face — and I remember how she would look up from across the room when she saw what I was up to, and how she would just stare at me, saying nothing but just watching me, the way a hunter might watch an animal at dusk, in the snow; or perhaps the way an animal might watch the hunter, who is moving so clumsily toward it, coming through the woods, right at dusk, with the animal wondering, Do I let him come closer? How much closer do I let him come? — while all the time her heart is beating, fluttering, and she knows, without knowing why, that even though it is dusk, and almost safe, that she has to run, must run, or suddenly all will come crashing down around her.

TITAN

THE SUMMER THAT I WITNESSED, breathed, lived the jubilee, I was twelve years old. My brother, Otto, who is four years older, was already on what he was calling the "fast track" to success, which he defined, and still does, as becoming rich. He is an investment banker, and I suppose it is fair to say that he has never known a moment's hardship. Even he refers to himself as *blessed*. I myself was never quite as comfortable in the presence of excessive bounty as he was.

Our parents were born in the heart of the Depression, grew up under its shadow, cowed and spooked I think by the fear and memory of it. Otto reacted by turning away from the cautious austerity of our parents, away from such fiscal and, some would say, emotional timidity, and struck out as soon as possible in the opposite direction, swimming hard and strong and eager for the profligate.

Our parents had worked hard establishing their own business as geologists — but it must have rankled Otto, as soon as he was old enough to notice such things: the way our parents held on to, and conserved, and reinvested their savings, setting aside safe and prudent amounts of it, as if against the coming storms of the world — storms that never came.

There was wealth almost everywhere in Texas in those days, and the fact that I have not participated in it since then, or rather, have chosen other kinds of wealth, does not mean that the monied type was unavailable to me. I simply was pulled in another direction. Even then, I had my own hungers, and still do.

They say that traits in a family, or even in a nation, are prone to sometimes skip generations, rising and falling in crests and troughs like waves far out beyond the Gulf. And although Otto was only four years older, I often felt as if I were an only child, that he was from the generation before me, and that my parents were from the generation before that generation, so that I was able to witness, and live between, the two ways of being in the world. And I do not mean to judge Otto — but whenever my parents would attempt to have a cautionary discussion with him about his hungry, consumptive ways, he would brush them off.

There was nothing that he did not see as a commodity, able to be bought or sold or traded, and leveraged or even stolen from the future. He was then and still is simply a taker, and it is the only way he is comfortable in the world: and though one day I suppose the world will run out of things to take and to trade — or rather, will run out of worthwhile things to take and trade — that is not quite yet the case, and I'd have to say that all in all he's continuing to live a fairly comfortable and satisfied life, and that he's more or less content, even in the continued savagery of his hunger. I think that he has found his own balance.

Though it did not occur to me when I was twelve, I came to realize later that our elderly parents — they would have been in their midfifties then — might have been a little awed by Otto, by the unquestioning force of his desire, the crisp efficiency of his gluttony, and by the power of his steadfast commitment, almost as if to a religious philosophy, to seek out anything rare and valuable, and purchase it, and count it, and market it: to acquire and consume.

Listening to him talk about such things — stocks and bonds, gold and silver, treasury notes and soybeans, cattle and poultry, coal and oil — was like watching a great predator gaze unblinkingly, its jaws parted, at a herd of unknowing grazing creatures. My parents weren't frightened of their oldest son, but they were awed. And who were they, besides his elders, to speak to him, to tell him that he was wrong, when they themselves had known a similar hunger but had simply grown up in a time when it seemed there was nothing available to acquire, and no means for the acquisition?

My own hunger was for a closeness, and a connection — a reduction in the vast and irreducible space I perceived to exist between all people, even within a family. It would have been fine with me if every morning the four of us had taken our breakfast together, and if the four of us had then gone out into the day to labor in the bright fields together, in some wholesome and ancient way, plowing and tilling, or harvesting and gathering, and to eat all our meals together then, and to end the day with a family reading, an hour or more of dramatic monologue, or a chautauqua.

Instead, we all sort of went our own ways, day after day. The closest we came to conventional or traditional or mythical unity was every summer when we went on vacation to a place in south Alabama, on the coast, called Point Clear. The hotel and resort where we stayed — the Grand Hotel — was elegant, even if the coast itself was hot and windy and muggy. In the evenings we would eat delicious seafood in the formal candlelit dining room, surrounded by other diners possessing far greater wealth than my parents': men and women who were no less than corporate titans. And each night, while I would sit there quietly, reflectively, dreaming a child's dreams, Otto would be looking all around, paying far more attention to the titans — to their mannerisms, and overheard conversations — than he did to the meal itself. And, even then, I would sometimes be aware of the manner in which my parents beheld both of us, and of their unspoken thoughts, as they wondered, *How can two brothers, or two of anything, turn out so different?* And I could see also that they were perturbed by this difference, this distance. As if we were all moving away from one another: as if our desire for space was the greatest gluttony.

At the hotel, each night was attended by endless opulence. We would all dress up, titans and nontitans, and enter that grand formal dining hall and be waited on, hand and foot, with one delicacy after another being brought to us, treats and treasures to be had merely for the asking, while a band played music at the other end of the hall. And the next day, after a breakfast of bright fruit and fresh juice, Otto and my parents would go off to play tennis or golf, while I would be on my own, free to wander the well-kept grounds, free to inhabit the reckless lands of my imagination. There was so much space.

I prowled the cattails in the water hazards along the golf

courses, catching fish and minnows and snakes and turtles and frogs — particularly the sleek and elegant spotted leopard frogs, which are already now nearly extinct. They were everywhere back then, and no one could ever have imagined they would simply, or not so simply, vanish. What other bright phenomena will vanish in our lifetimes, becoming one day merely memory and story, tale and legacy, and then fragments of story and legacy, and then nothing, only wind?

I spent the middle of the afternoons sitting in the air-conditioned lobby, playing chess with and against myself, bare-chested in my damp swimsuit, sitting on a leather sofa with sand grains crumbling from between my toes onto the cool tile floor. I ordered root beer and grilled cheese sandwiches from the pool, charging them to our room, and in my concentration on the game I would spill potato chips into the folds of the leather furniture. I failed to notice the icy looks that must have been coming from the desk clerks.

There are so many different types of gluttony. Even now, just as when I was a child and without responsibility, I can lie on my back in the tall grass in autumn and stare at the clouds, an adult with not a thought in my head; and when I stand up, hours later, I will still be ravenous for the sight of those clouds, and for the whispering of that grass, and when I go to bed that night I will still be hungry for the memory of the warmth of that late-season sun, even as, in the moment, I am enjoying the scent and embrace of the darkness, and the cooling night.

At Point Clear, we'd meet up again for dinner — Otto and my parents tanned from the extravagances of their own day, and relaxed: appearing not quite sated — never that — but almost. Even then I felt acutely that I was between two lands.

I wanted to take but I also wanted to give: though what, I wasn't sure.

Were there others like me? I had no idea. It was entirely possible that I was alone in this regard: that even amid bounty, too much space surrounded me.

The jubilee was a phenomenon that usually happened only once every few summers in south Alabama, following afternoon thunderstorms in the upland part of the state. The storms would drop several inches of rain into all the creeks and streams and rivers in a short period of time. That surge of fresh cold rainwater would then come rushing down toward the Gulf, gaining speed and potency, doubling at every confluence, until finally, a few hours later — almost always in the middle of the night — the wall of fresh water would come rolling into the Gulf.

The moon was involved with the jubilee, too, though I don't know exactly how. Perhaps the moon had to be full, and pulling out a big rip tide just when all the extra fresh water came gushing out — or maybe it was the other way around, and the moon had to be bringing a high tide of seawater upriver — but anyway, the bottom line, or so said the brochure I had read at the front desk, was that when the jubilee hit the flush of fresh water would stun or kill all the saltwater fish in the vicinity, and that the fresh water would also carry out on its plume a swirling mix of freshwater creatures — catfish, gar, crawdads, bullfrogs — that would also be salt-stunned.

It was a rare thing, almost a once-in-a-lifetime thing, to see it. I made sure our family's name was on the list for the wake-up call. The first year I signed us up, I was seven years old. I'd lie there in our cottage every night, watching the moon through the window, waiting for the phone to ring. The woman at the front desk told me that whenever you answered the phone and heard the one word — "Jubilee!" — it meant the thing was on.

I would lie awake wondering if it had rained in the uplands that day. I would strain my ears to see if I could hear the shouts of "Jubilee!" drifting across the golf course, and up and down the beach.

Summer after summer passed in this manner, with me wandering solitary along the edges of the bright and well-kept lawns and gardens of wealth in the daytime, and lying there in the cottage each night, trying to stay awake for as long as I could, awaiting the call.

I imagined that the jubilee was an event of such significance that the hotel staff kept someone down at the beach each night on permanent lookout, like a lifeguard perched high in a chair, waiting to report its arrival.

In the summer when I was eleven, finally, the call did come, but I was asleep, and didn't find out about it until weeks later, when we were back home. The phone had rung at two A.M., and when my father leaned over and picked up the phone, a woman's voice cried "Jubilee!" and then hung up. Neither my father nor my mother had a clue what a jubilee was, much less that I had signed us up for one.

The year that I was twelve — the year I finally saw the jubilee — I slept by the phone. It was very rare to have two jubilees in two years — and this time I got to the phone, and got to hear the woman say it.

She uttered just that one word — *Jubilee!* — and then hung up. I hurried outside, and could see other people al-

ready moving down toward the beach in the moonlight —
some in bathrobes, others in shorts and sandals. Some had
flashlights, though the moon was so bright you didn't really
need one.

I went back inside and got my family up. At first they
didn't want to go, but I kept haranguing them, and finally
they awakened.

By the time we made it down to the water, people were already wading out into the ocean. The first thing that hit me
— beyond the beauty of the moonlight on the water — was
the scent of fresh fish.

It wasn't quite as I had pictured it would be. I had imagined that there might be a thousand people, or even ten
thousand; but instead there were only about forty of us,
moving slowly through the waves, our heads down, searching for the stunned fish floating belly-up. I had thought people would hear about it on the radio stations, and through
word of mouth, and that there would be cars parked all up
and down the beach — that people would have come all the
way from Mobile and Pensacola, and even farther: Biloxi,
Hattiesburg, and the uplands — Selma, Columbus, and Tal-
lahassee. But instead it was just us: the resort-goers.

I had thought you would be able to see the jubilee, too —
that the plume of fresh water would be darker, like spilled
ink, and that you would be able to discern precisely where it
entered and mixed with the bay, being diluted and spread
laterally by the longshore currents. But it wasn't that way
at all. I couldn't tell any difference between salt water and
fresh. The waters looked just as they always had. Every now
and then I could catch the faintest whiff of something really
fresh and dark — organic, like black dirt, forest, nutmeat,

rotting bark — but always, just as soon as I became aware of that dark little thread of scent, it would disappear, absorbed by the mass of the ocean.

I had thought there would be more fish, too. I had thought there would be millions. Instead, there were only thousands. Some of the smaller ones appeared dead, but the larger ones were just stunned, swimming sideways or upside down, gasping and confused. They were out there for as far as I could see — white bellies shining in the moonlight — and other fish were careening as if drunk against my legs — fish panicked, fish drowning, is what it looked and felt like — and people carried pillowcases and plastic bags over their shoulders, filling them as if they were gathering squash or potatoes from a garden.

Everyone participated. Class distinctions fell away, and Otto and my mother and father and I loaded our pillowcases right alongside the rich and the superrich, as well as alongside the hotel workers, filling our pillowcases with our catches: crabs, catfish, red snapper, flounder, shrimp, bullfrogs, sheepshead, angelfish . . . We didn't have to worry about sharks, because they wouldn't come in to where the fresh water was mixing. It was all ours. For that one night — or those few hours — it was all ours. Father and Mother were very happy, as were all of the people out on the beach, and it felt to me as if I had been drawn already into some other, older world — the land of adults — without having quite yet petitioned for or having even desired such entrance, still pleased as I was by childhood.

In remembering the jubilee, I recall how different the quality of sound was. It wasn't extraordinarily loud; it was just different, a combination of sounds I had never heard before.

The waves were shushing and the confused fish were slapping the water as they thrashed and fought the poison of the fresh water. There were a lot of birds overhead, gulls mostly, squalling and squealing, and the ten-piece band from the restaurant had come down and set up along the water's edge, and they were playing.

The hotel staff had set up dining tables with linen tablecloths out on the beach, and they had lit torches and candles all along the shore, and around the dining tables. The chefs had come down to the jubilee also, and the chefs were chopping off fish heads and gutting the entrails, slicing off filets and frying and boiling and grilling a dozen different recipes at once, luminous in their bright white aprons, knives flashing in the candlelight. There were cats everywhere, cats coming from out of the sea oats to take those fish heads and run back off into the bushes with them.

There was a boy walking up and down the beach, staying almost always just at the farthest edge of the light from the candles and lanterns and bonfires. He was barefoot, like all of us, and shirtless, and was wearing blue jeans that had been cut off at the knees; and as he paced back and forth, observing us, I could tell that he was agitated. His agitation stood out even more, surrounded as he was by the almost somnolent contentedness of everyone else. The rest of us sloshed around in the waves, our heads tipped slightly downward like wading birds', with all the fish in the world available to us, it seemed, just for the taking.

The boy was roughly my age, and because he was hanging back at the edge of firelight, back in the blue-silver light of the moon, that is how I thought of him, as the blue boy. I hadn't seen him around earlier in the week, and I had the feeling that rather than a hotel guest he was some feral way-farer who had wandered down our way from a distant, ragged shack back in the palmetto bushes.

He looked hungry, too — like those cats that kept dragging away the fish heads — and though I couldn't hear any voices over the little lapping sounds of the surf, I got the impression that he would sometimes call out to us, asking for something, and I avoided observing him too closely, out of concern that he might somehow seek me out.

Once the chefs had most of the fish prepared, they began ringing a series of large copper bells mounted on heavy wrought-iron stands and tripods, and as that gonging carillon rolled out across the waves, most of us turned and waded back to shore, to seat ourselves at the long dining tables set up in the sand; though still a few people remained out in the water. Some of them had borrowed tools from the gardener's shed and were raking in the fish, or shoveling them into baskets — unwilling to stop, even when the feast was ready and waiting, and set before them.

We ate and ate. The chefs mixed champagne and orange juice in pitchers for us at sunrise and blew out the torches. We could see the fish out in the ocean starting to recover when the sun came up. The surface of the water was thrashing again as fish spun and flopped and rolled back over, right side up.

The blue boy had disappeared when the thirty or so of us had turned and come marching back in from out of the waves; but now he reappeared, came out into the soft gray light of dawn, and I could see that my initial impression had been correct, that he was scraggly and feral, as rough as a cob; and that indeed he was agitated, for now he waded out into the waves and began scolding the dozen or so guests who were still out there with pitchforks and shovels and bushel-baskets and trash cans, still raking in those stressed and wounded and compromised fish. He was hollering at them also to leave the biggest, healthiest fish, and was shouting at them to come on in, that they had taken enough, had taken more than enough.

With the boy's attention focused elsewhere, I was free to observe him without being noticed, and there was something about him that made me think that he was not from this country — though what other country he might have been from, I could not have said. A country, I supposed, where they had run out of fish.

The pitchforkers ignored the blue boy, however, and kept on reaching for more and more fish, stabbing and spearing them, scooping and netting them into their baskets, until finally all the fish were gone and the sun was bright in the sky: and the blue boy just stood there, staring at them, nearly chest deep in the waves, and then he turned and made his way back to shore, and disappeared into the dunes.

The sun rose orange over the water, and the ocean turned foggy gray, the same color as the sky. The band stopped playing, the waiters and waitresses cleared the tables, and we all went back to our rooms to sleep.

For two days afterward we would see all these rich people who'd come to this place for a vacation working on their fish instead. They kept them cool in garbage cans filled with ice, and would be scaling and filleting fish all day long: these bankers and lawyers and doctors and titans. Some of them used electric knives, and we'd hear that buzzing, humming sound, a sawing, going on all day.

They were slipping with the knives and chopping up their hands, so that at dinner the next couple of nights we would see people trying to eat with their hands wrapped in gauze bandages, with blood splotches soaking through them.

The rich people would have fish scales all over them, too — not a lot, just one or two: stuck to a thumbnail or sometimes a cheekbone, or in their hair — and they wouldn't realize it, so that the scales would be glittering as they ate. It made them look special, as if they were wearing some new kind of jewelry, or as if they were on their way to a party or had just come from one.

We ate fish for breakfast, lunch, and dinner. They were far and away the best fish I've ever eaten. The clerk in the lobby said she'd actually been disappointed by the yield — that it was one of the briefest and smallest jubilees she'd witnessed yet — and when I asked about the blue boy who'd been so upset, she said that he lived just a mile or so up the beach and that he was always there during a jubilee, and that in years past his father and grandfather had been there also, shouting the same things.

She said his was a fishing family, and that his warnings were not to be taken seriously, that they probably just wanted all the fish for themselves. Still, she admitted, the jubilees *were* getting smaller by the year, and less and less frequent. She said the blue boy came from a large family; she guessed that he had at least a dozen brothers and sisters, and that they were all churchgoers, fundamentalists, and very close, like some kind of old-fashioned feudal clan. She said that if you crossed one of them, you brought down the wrath of all of them, and that it was best to steer clear of them. She said they were all alike, that there wasn't a hair's breadth of difference between any of them.

For the next couple of days Otto and I got up early and went back down to the beach just before daylight, to see if by some freak chance the jubilee might be happening again, if even on a lesser scale — like a shadow of the jubilee. We went down to the beach and waded out into the ocean. The water was dark, and the sky was dark — once or twice a mullet skipped across the surface — but that was it. Things were back to the way they had been before, big and empty.

It was almost kind of restful, standing there in the ocean without all the noise and excitement. Or it was for me, anyway. How was I to know then that Otto, standing right next to me, was looking at the same ocean in an entirely different way? That he wanted another jubilee right away, and then another, and another.

"That fucking boy," he said, speaking of the blue boy. "We weren't hurting anything. The ocean is filled with fish, *overflowing* with fish," Otto said. "The whole world could eat that many fish every day, and the new fish being born into the ocean each day would be filling their places faster than we could eat them. We could drag one giant net from here to China, and by the time we had crossed the ocean the waters behind us would have filled back in with fish, so that we could turn around and go back in the other direction, filling our nets again and again."

I saw that it was important for him to believe this, so I said nothing. But there was nothing in the ocean that day, and neither, I am told, was there ever another jubilee at Point Clear. We were witnesses to the last one. We were participants in the last one. I do not think we were to blame for its being the last one, and neither do I think that if people had listened to the blue boy things would have turned out differently. I think there are too many other factors, but I also think there was too much gluttony, and not enough humility.

I can understand the nature of gluttony. I think it is the nature of the terrible truth these days — that there is not quite enough of almost everything, or anything. Or maybe one thing — one gentle, unconnected thing — though what that thing might be, or rather, the specificity of it, I could not say.

We left for home on the third day following the jubilee. We wrapped all our leftover fish in plastic bags and newspapers and put them in boxes with ice in the trunk and drove through the night to stay out of the day's heat. The ice kept melting, so fish-water was trickling out the back the whole way home. Every time we stopped for gas, we'd buy new bags of ice. But we got the fish home, and into the deep freeze. They lasted for about a year.

Otto has been living in New York City for more than thirty years now. I still live in Texas, along the Gulf Coast, and miss him, and it has been a long time now since we've been out in the woods, or the ocean, together. Our parents eventually died, without seeing another jubilee, though we went back to that same vacation spot again and again for many years afterward. All that remains of the jubilee is my own and a few others' dimming memories of it.

When I remember the jubilee, and those days of childhood, what I think about now is not so much the fish made so easily available to us, or the music of the big band, or the candlelight feast, but rather the way all of us converged on one place, one time, with one goal, even if that goal was to serve ourselves, rather than others.

Even if we were ferocious in our consumption, we were connected, that night, and those next few days. We were like a larger family, and there was bounty in the world, and the security of bounty, and no divisiveness or hierarchies, only the gift of bounty, all the bounty that the land and the sea could deliver to us, and with us never even having to ask or work for it.

It was like childhood. Nothing, and no one, had yet been separated from anything else — not for any reason. I am glad that I saw it, and though this in itself might seem a childlike wish, I find myself imagining some days that we might all yet see it again.

The Book of Yaak

Bass delves into the soul of one of the last great wild places in the United States, the Yaak Valley of northwestern Montana.

ISBN 978-0-395-87746-3

Colter: The True Story of the Best Dog I Ever Had

Bass captures the essence of canine companionship with this vivid account of his relationship with Colter, a German shorthair pup.

ISBN 978-0-618-12736-8

The Diezmo: A Novel

This novel offers a stirring account of the Mier Expedition, one of the most absurd and tragic military adventures in American history.

ISBN 978-0-618-71050-8

The Hermit's Story: Stories

Selected as a Los Angeles Times Book of the Year, this collection explores the connections between man and nature.

ISBN 978-0-618-38044-2

In the Loyal Mountains: Stories

Each of these ten dazzling short stories embraces vibrant images of ordinary life and exuberant descriptions of nature.

ISBN 978-0-395-87747-0

The Lives of Rocks: Stories

Finalist for the Story Prize, this collection features exquisite stories set in Montana, Texas, and Mississippi.

ISBN 978-0-618-91966-6

The Lost Grizzlies: A Search for Survivors in the Wilderness of Colorado

Bass describes the courage, hope, and friendships at the heart of the search for grizzlies in the San Juan Mountains.

ISBN 978-0-395-85700-7

The Ninemile Wolves

Following the fate of a modern wolf pack, Bass charts the deeply conflicted relationship between man and beast.

ISBN 978-0-618-26302-8

The Sky, the Stars, the Wilderness: Novellas

Magical, passionate, and lyrical, this collection of three novellas received the Mountains and Plains Booksellers Award for Fiction.

ISBN 978-0-395-92475-4

Where the Sea Used to Be: A Novel

Bass's first full-length novel is the story of a struggle between a father and his daughter for the souls of two men—his protégés, her lovers.

ISBN 978-0-395-95781-3

Winter: Notes from Montana

In a celebration of winter in a remote, sparsely populated valley of Montana, Bass describes the slow-motion quality of life and the dangers of the wilderness.

ISBN 978-0-395-61150-0

www.marinerbooks.com